1

Chapter One - Thursday 18th October

Sarah excused herself from her four panellists sitting around the presentation table and hurried through into the small adjoining kitchen. So far, Olga, Margaret, Ayesha, and Jason had arrived. She prayed the last two people wouldn't be too late as the quiche tarts took twenty-five minutes to cook. Placing the five varieties of tarts onto baking trays she set the oven timer and just as she closed the oven door, she heard a man's voice calling, hello.

Hurrying back through to the small square room she welcomed the second man of the group. She was expecting a man aged forty-one and thought it best to check his name. 'Hi, are you, Mark Whittaker?'

'Yep, that's me,' he said holding out his hand to shake.

This guy, in his jeans and stripy cream shirt looked much younger and more like mid-thirties. He wasn't particularly good looking with a large nose, moustache, and short-trimmed, goatee-beard but when she shook his hand, Sarah felt a frisson of heat surge through her. She caught her breath. How strange was that? She hadn't had thoughts about men for over six months, well, not since Paul had walked out.

The huge grin he gave her reached from one ear to another and seemed to light up his whole face. While she held onto his hand, he raised a quizzical eyebrow.

Sarah realised she was staring at him and shook herself back to reality and showed him to his seat around the table. She reached up and opened the only small window in the room and laid her hand on the old radiator which was belting out heat.

While Mark started to greet the other panellists the door to the room opened and banged shut.

A woman's loud voice exclaimed, 'Blooming traffic! It's taken forever to get through the rush hour, and parking, well don't start me off on that one!'

Sarah surmised this must be her last panellist. 'Hello, and you must be Rebecca Jones?' She said, 'Come and join us at the table and we'll make our introductions.'

Mumbling apologies Rebecca took a seat next to Mark and Sarah noticed how she also looked at him appreciatively. Mark turned and treated Rebecca to one of his lovely smiles and she felt a stab of envy.

Scolding herself she pushed all thoughts of men from her mind, pulled her shoulders back and began her introductory talk. She welcomed everyone to the first of ten weekly sessions which would run up to Christmas.

'And to tempt your tastebuds,' she said. 'We'll be sampling, cocktail sausages, turkey crowns, trifles, prawn cocktails, custard, sausage rolls, Christmas cakes and puddings. In fact, these make up most of our popular selling products at Christmas time and the last panel will be on Thursday 20th December.'

There was a general buzz of excitement with exclamations of ooh and aah.

Sarah gave them a few minutes to settle then continued, 'So, we are lucky here in North Shields to have one of the large supermarkets and our retailer values their customers opinions. I'll note down all the results and your comments which will be sent to head office for consideration. This information helps the buying and marketing teams keep abreast of what their competitors have on their shelves. Therefore, each week we'll have samples from M&S, Tesco, Waitrose, Sainsbury's, and Asda, to taste. And, of course you'll all be given your £25 voucher at the end of each session to spend as you like. It's our way of thanking you for taking the time to come and give us your feedback.'

Taking a deep breath, she stared straight into Mark's deep brown eyes. He was sitting directly opposite gazing at her with a smile playing around his lips. She shuffled on the hard plastic chair while handing out her welcome packs.

Lowering his gaze, Mark took brown-legged glasses out of his shirt pocket and placed them onto his nose.

The square, clear lenses transformed his eyes and make them look bigger and darker. She looked again at his thick brown hair and decided that along with his brilliant smile, he was indeed, incredibly good looking.

Sitting on the other side to Mark was one of two older ladies.

Olga, had a loud high-pitched tone to her voice when she asked, 'And what do we do if there's something on the session that we don't like? I don't think I've eaten a cocktail sausage in my life.'

Sarah dragged her eyes from Mark. 'Good question, Olga,' she said. 'Just let me know. And if there's something you don't want to eat you only need to fill in the appearance, and aroma section of the form which I'll go through later. Now, as we are going to spend a couple of hours together every night for the next ten weeks, I usually find it helpful to spend five minutes introducing ourselves.'

The other elderly lady said, 'Oh, dear, I'm not particularly good at talking in front of people.'

Sarah smiled reassuringly and leaned across the table to cover Margaret's fluttering hands with one of her own. 'That's fine, please don't worry,' she said. 'Everyone, this is Margaret Atkinson. She lives on Camp Terrace and has signed up for the taste panel because…' Sarah nodded encouragingly at Margaret until she realised that she was to continue with the sentence.

'O…oh, well,' Margaret said. 'I do love eating food and cooking. And although I'm on my own now, if either of my sons come to visit at Christmas, I would like to have plenty of food in the pantry, so the vouchers will be handy for the Two for One Deals.'

Sarah beamed at her. 'Hey, that's a great idea, Margaret,' she said squeezing her hand.

Everyone around the table smiled encouragingly at Margaret.

Everyone except Olga, who with large arms folded under her heavy bust gave a loud, 'Hmph!' Through thin pursed lips, she said, 'It must be at least three years since you've seen either of them, Margaret.'

Margaret's shoulders rounded and she put her head down staring at the table.

Sarah heard Rebecca click her tongue in annoyance at Olga's rude comment.

To try and smooth over the situation, she turned to Mark. 'So, how about you, Mark? Why did you decide to come along?'

Mark winked at her, and she knew he'd worked out her distraction technique. He sat forward with his hands folded on the table. 'Well, some of you might know my face as I own the photography and art studio on the high street.'

Margaret raised her head again and exclaimed, 'Ah, I thought I recognised your face when you came into the room but wasn't certain.'

Mark smiled back at her. 'Yep, that's me. Some of you might have known my late wife, Jessie who died two years ago,' he said. 'I've found it hard getting used to cooking for one again. However, I'm determined to try and eat more healthily, and have bought Jamie Oliver's fast supper cookbook. I intend to spend my vouchers on spices and herbs. So, who knows, I might become the next celebrity chef!'

He gave a throaty laugh. His cheeks were pink as though embarrassed at his open admission about his wife. The reaction around the table was electric.

Olga's eyebrows shot up in surprise and Sarah could tell she was trying to remember if she knew him or Jessie.

'Oh, you, poor mite,' Margaret muttered softly.

It looked as if Rebecca was digesting the news that he was a widower with relish and leant towards him then squeezed his shoulder.

Sarah stared at her long, red-polished fingernails in envy.

Mark turned to Rebecca and smiled then nodded his thanks.

Sarah decided to draw the last two panellists, who had so far been watching and listening, into the conversation.

'Thanks, Mark,' she said and turned away to look at the other male in the group, Jason Smith. 'Now, what brings you along, Jason?'

Jason's small but pleasing face looked a little startled. He grinned at everyone revealing a large gap between his two front teeth. 'Well, I'm what is fashionably known as a house-husband to my twin daughters who are nine months old. My, wife, Stacey, works in the estate agents and when she arrives home, and we've had dinner, she baths and beds the little darlings and I get a couple of hours grace. We'll be spending the vouchers on nappies, talcum powder and baby food, I'm afraid.'

He pulled a comical face and Margaret clapped her hands together with a big grin on her face. 'Oooh, twin babies,' she said, 'How lovely!'

While Sarah had been listening to Jason's soft voice, she decided that he didn't sound like the usual alpha male. And when he'd first arrived in very tight skinny jeans with a satchel slung across his jumper, she'd wondered about him.

Then reminded herself how wrong it was to make assumptions on first appearances.

Mark hooted. 'Oh my, well if you want to share a case of red wine, your secret will be safe with me!'

Jason guffawed, and she could see the two men begin to bond.

With experience of doing these tasting panels, Sarah had become an expert of watching group interactions. She knew as the weeks passed, they'd all get to know one another better and relax in each other's company.

Sitting next to Jason was the most beautiful Indian girl Sarah had ever seen. The red tunic she wore with a gold sparkle woven into the pattern seemed to glisten in the sun which shone through the window behind her. Until now, Ayesha had sat with her head bent and eyes lowered throughout the introductions. It was only now when she looked up at Sarah from huge, brown, oval shaped eyes that Sarah appreciated how stunningly beautiful she really was.

Sarah smiled. 'Ayesha, would you like to go next. But before you start can I just say your tunic is fabulous! Those colours are so striking together.'

Her shoulders lifted. 'Thanks, Sarah,' she said, 'I made it myself.'

Margaret said, 'Oh, how clever of you, dear. You are obviously very talented; whereas I can't even sew a button on!'

A slight titter of laughter escaped Rebecca's lips, but she added, 'I quite agree, it's absolutely stunning.'

Sarah asked Ayesha, 'And you wanted to come along, because?'

Ayesha's cheeks flushed and she lifted her chin. 'Well, I'm eighteen and I want to save the vouchers to buy myself a kindle to read my favourite books. My, home is above our corner shop where I live with my parents and my two brothers who are twelve and fourteen.'

Olga squinted and in her imperial voice she asked, 'And are you made to work in the shop, dear?'

Sarah saw Ayesha bristle then look down at Olga's name card. 'No, Mrs Treadcott,' she said. 'I work as a receptionist at the medical centre.'

Good for you, Sarah thought, that's put Olga back in her place. Ayesha had done it with respect and impeccable manners.

Before Sarah could ask Rebecca to speak next, Olga interrupted. 'Surely it must be my turn now?'

Sarah smiled and nodded her consent.

Olga pulled her broad shoulders back and licked her lips which were smeared in a scarlet red lipstick. 'I'm Mrs Treadcott, and I have a three bedroomed detached property on Cleveland Road. My, husband, when he was alive, was a senior civil servant for the ministry of transport, therefore, we were what one would call well-travelled. I'm on the resident's association, and I wanted to come along to keep abreast of what is happening in our community. And, to make sure ordinary people are not being taken advantage of by this company.'

Olga looked at her as if to say and I'm keeping my eye on you. But Sarah wasn't intimated by Olga Treadcott. She'd been doing consumer research for years and had met people from all levels of society. She was confident in her professionalism and her ability to run the group session.

She saw Olga take a deep breath as if to speak again, but Sarah cut her short. 'Thanks, Olga, that's great,' she said. 'And now, last but certainly not least, Rebecca?'

Sarah turned back to face Mark and Rebecca. She was pleased that Rebecca was sitting down because she looked at least five foot nine and with two-inch wedged heels she would have towered above her measly height of five foot three. She had to admit that Rebecca was an extremely attractive woman with long, black, sleek hair tied up in a high ponytail which swished from side to side when she moved her head.

Rebecca folded her hands calmly and confidently in her lap, gave everyone a sincere smile and said, 'Yes, I'm Rebecca Jones, I'm forty-three, and divorced. I'm a lawyer and associate on Northumberland Square, although I do work from home most of the time. And yes, Olga, I do know where your house is, but my five bedroomed detached property is on Preston Road overlooking the park.'

Sarah could see Rebecca pause to wait for reaction around the table. Olga wrinkled her nose in the air then patted the back of her bouffant hairstyle. Sarah was delighted with Rebecca's put down because everyone would know that her house was practically double the price of Olga's.

Rebecca continued, 'And I'm going on my first holiday to Italy next year so thought I'd use the vouchers to try some new pasta dishes.'

'Fab idea, Rebecca,' Jason said nodding.

Mark smiled. 'I've been to Venice and Rome,' he said. 'You'll love the country.'

Sarah stood up. 'That's great everyone. Now I'll give you two quick minutes about me before I rescue the tarts from the oven. My, name is Sarah Williams and I'm 36. I was born here in Preston village and went to Northumbria University to do a food science degree then got my first job with this supermarket chain at their head office in London. I worked there for years as a sensory analyst and have returned home now to live and run the food section. I have a department of three juniors to supervise and due to the popularity of our Tuesday night taste panel I decided to start this extra Thursday session because we have a back-log of products to assess before Christmas.'

She began to walk towards the kitchen and heard the group interact together. Jason and Ayesha began to talk, and she heard Rebecca ask Mark about his studio.

The oven timer bleeped, and she checked the central temperature of the tarts with a probe. They were fully cooked, and she put them onto five plates with random numbers marked on the side. There was a small serving hatch in the wall between the two rooms and she opened the two flaps to put the plates through. Picking up the first two plates she looked up to see Mark's face on the room side of the hatch.

'Can I help?' he asked grinning at her.

He really was nice, she thought nodding then handed the plates through to him. Settled back at the table Sarah asked everyone to open the packs and explained the sensory forms with columns for scores and comments relating to appearance, aroma, texture, and flavour.

Cutting each tart into six pieces, she said, 'And if I could just ask that you don't talk and discuss anything while completing the forms that would be great. We can discuss it all later at the end. Discussions influence separate opinions because everyone has their own taste and it's what you all think individually that counts.'

The smell of cooked pastry and cheese filled the room and she smiled. 'Now, just a few pointers with these quiche tarts,' she said. 'Pay particular attention to the pastry. Is it crisp or is it soggy on the bottom of the tart? Also, please take note of the flavours in the filling. Is there too much ham overpowering the cheese, or vice versa? Or is the combination exactly right.'

Everyone nodded in understanding, and she asked them to start tasting each sample then record their scores.

After she'd helped Margaret with a couple of questions, she pretended to read her paperwork, but she was watching Mark. He must have been devastated to lose his wife so young, she thought. She wondered whether he was content on his own. Or was he lonely and ready to accept Rebecca's obvious flirtations. They would make a lovely couple being both attractive and professional, she thought, and seemed to have their pasts well and truly behind them.

Whereas she couldn't claim that her turbulent break-up from Paul was completely behind her. It was only six months since he'd announced that he had fallen in love with an Italian model and was moving to Milan. And how, after nine happy years of living together, they could manage the end of their relationship in a mature and sensible manner. It had been at this stage that she'd snapped and hurled a saucepan at him. He'd ran from their apartment, and she'd never seen him since. Earlier, when Rebecca had mentioned Italy, she had felt her insides twist with painful association.

Mark suddenly looked up and smiled at her. Had he known that she'd been staring at him? He gave her a slight nod of his head and she smiled back. It looked as though he was enjoying himself.

When everyone had finished Sarah collected the forms and did a quick calculation declaring which sample was the winning tart. She read out the comments then announced the panel's worst tart sample and the reasons why. Everyone chattered excitedly agreeing with each other.

Sarah said, 'So, on this panel we've had good decisive results because all six of you agree but going forwards, there may be some products where the differences might not be so clear cut and it could be harder to reach a conclusive result.'

Everyone nodded and she smiled at them all around the table. 'Well, thanks to you all and I hope you've enjoyed the first session.'

She placed the six vouchers on the table. 'Hopefully, I'll see you all next week at the same time.'

Sarah noticed Olga was the first to snap up her voucher from the table and that the others followed at a slower pace.

'Yes, I'll definitely be here,' Mark said smiling. 'I've really enjoyed it.'

There was agreement from everyone, and chairs were scraped back then jackets and coats put on. They certainly looked a different mix of characters, Sarah thought as they filed out of the room. Her Tuesday session was made up of all middle-aged housewives, but these Thursday sessions were certainly going to be different. And very interesting indeed, she mused.

Chapter Two – Friday 19th October

Mark ran down the stairs from the tasting room buzzing after the most interesting couple of hours he'd had for a long while. He had never dreamt that he would enjoy it so much. Reaching the bottom of the office block and into the car park he thought of the seven people he'd just spent time with, especially Sarah and Rebecca.

Both women were different in their own way, and he was surprised at how much he'd enjoyed their company. It was a whole new experience for him because he'd only ever been with Jessie, childhood sweethearts since he was sixteen years old. His confidence with women however was in his boots, or in this case, he thought looking down at his feet, his Italian leather loafers. He turned the ignition of his red Yaris and left the car park.

Unless he was very much mistaken, Rebecca was coming on to him and although she was extremely attractive, available, and an intelligent lady she was a little scary. If only he could start gradually with a friendship, then progress to dating he'd feel much happier.

He sighed but had the feeling Rebecca wasn't the type of woman to take anything slowly. Still, the little she'd told him about her job was interesting, she was well-travelled, and very independent.

Driving towards the edge of town he then thought of Sarah. From the minute he'd shook her hand and looked into those big blue eyes he had felt a tingle run through his whole body. And by the look on her face, he was sure she had felt it too.

When she'd talked to the group he had been entranced and couldn't take his eyes from her. She appeared gentle and quietly spoken but very professional at the same time. She had been kind and understanding with Margaret and Ayesha who were obviously introvert characters and nervous in a group situation. He'd seen her make them feel relaxed and comfortable which was a great achievement.

He turned into the corner of Preston Gate to his bungalow and felt the previous euphoria flatten. The usual unhappiness settled upon him like a black cloud. It was always like this now. He hated the place.

It wasn't just because Jessie was gone, and his home was empty and lonely but more the appearance. From, the outside ramp, to the handrail, the layout of the rooms, and general feeling of an old person's residence that he hated. They'd chosen it when Jessie couldn't walk any longer, and a wheelchair-friendly home was necessary.

Closing the garage door, he happily thought of their old terraced, two up, two down house in Preston Village then smiled with the memories. They'd been newly-weds, were young and in love, and he'd loved going home to Jessie every night.

Sam, his cocker-spaniel barked his hello as he turned the key and opened the door to a tumultuous reception. Collecting the post from the mat he ruffled the dog's neck wondering if he too missed the old house. But that was daft, he sighed, because Sam would never leave his side wherever they lived.

He'd bought Sam after Jessie had miss-carried their first baby girl at six months and she'd screamed at him. 'So, you think bringing a puppy home will take away the pain of losing my baby?'

He had been crestfallen. 'No, of course not. And she wasn't just your baby she was my daughter too.'

Then the following year they'd lost a baby boy in another miscarriage, and he'd had to fight to keep their marriage together. Having Sam to walk twice a day had kept him sane. It had been time out away from Jessie because as the months passed, she'd blamed him for everything. Most days when they'd been home together, she was horrible towards him, but this was the side to Jessie that only he'd ever seen. The smiley happy side to Jessie was painted on with her lipstick in the mirror every morning. Everyone thought she was a star.

Sam trotted along next to his legs and into the kitchen where he filled his bowl with favourite dog food and biscuit then wondered what to cook for his own dinner. It was nearly eight, but because he'd eaten the quiche tarts, he wasn't hungry. He decided to settle for cheese and biscuits later. Pulling the voucher from his pocket he laid it on the bench remembering Sarah's soft blonde hair and those lovely eyes.

At one stage during the session, he'd thought she was staring at him, and they'd caught each other with eye-to-eye contact. But surely not, he thought. A woman like that was bound to have a partner. She was too gorgeous to be on her own and although she wore no ring on her finger, he supposed that meant nothing these days.

***

Ellen, his part time assistant was opening the shop for him this morning, so he decided to have his bowl of healthy breakfast cereal and take his Friday morning at a slower pace. Later when he entered the shop, he called good morning and with a spring in his step he crossed the floor to the cash desk then hung his jacket on the back of the door.

'Wow!' Ellen said looking up from the ledger. 'You look good this morning.'

He grinned and stood next to her. 'Yeah, I had a good night and enjoyed the supermarket panel. We tasted quiche tarts and it was amazing how different they all were, and how we all thought the same about the flavour and appearance. The pieces of ham in the best one was particularly good quality, and the flavour was really lovely.'

Ellen shook her copper-red curls. 'Ah, don't, you're making me hungry. I'm just thinking about nipping out for a bacon bap, do you want one?'

'Why not,' he said grinning. 'I'm supposed to be starting my healthy eating diet, but I can start on Monday instead. I'll shop over the weekend and get organised for next week.'

While Ellen pulled on her denim jacket and took a £5 note from the till, he looked at the ledger from the previous day. The monthly takings were good and had slowly been increasing all year until he was now turning over a great profit. Compared to the previous few years this was nothing short of a miracle.

During the year he'd had to nurse Jessie through her later stages and subsequent death had meant the takings were so low there was days when it hadn't been worth opening the studio. He prayed the profit would continue because it was the only way he could make enough money to sell the bungalow and buy an apartment on Quayside Court with the fabulous views. His dream of moving out of the depressing bungalow was all he could think of some days. And knew the day he walked away from it would be the day he left the past behind forever.

Going through to the small kitchenette he switched on the kettle and thought of how he'd changed the product range he was selling. Now the shelves were stocked with specialist pens and pencils, paper and card, sketch and notebooks, camera and camcorder film, and all manner of drawing and painting inks. He also knew this change was partly due to Ellen and her exuberance for all things arty. And for life itself.

He remembered the day she had bounced into the shop asking if he could give her a job.

'Hiya,' she'd said. 'I'm at Uni doing my art degree and looking for a part-time job. I need to make extra cash. You know us students, we never have enough money!'

She had laughed and humped a huge Mary Poppins bag onto the desk. She'd lifted a folder out with black & white sketches of the new quayside development and had talked him through each one.

She had gabbled at ninety miles an hour about how hard she would work and what changes they could make then asked, 'And have you ever thought of including photography in your portfolio and some modern framing techniques?'

He had thrown his hands up in defeat. 'Okay,' he'd said. 'But sometimes I have trouble selling my own art works never mind someone else's. So, I can't promise you sales on your work.'

She'd smiled and her young green eyes had sparkled with delight. 'That's fine. I don't expect that. But if you could pay me minimum wage to help serve and run the shop that would be great. It'll be much better than working in a pub pulling pints.'

And so, she'd brought her happy-go-lucky personality into the shop two or three times a week and he knew after Jessie's death it had given him a new lease of life. They'd started to dabble in photography, and cartoon drawings, trendy posters, framing canvas prints and changed the traditional art shop layout into a contemporary art and photography area.

In one corner they'd created a small six-foot section of wall to photograph headshots and had lightweight, portable supports, and light stands. He was extraordinarily proud of the transformation and had eased his love of painting to the side and was now all consumed with the photography side of the business which had in turn, increased his weekly profit margin beyond all his dreams.

Just as he carried two coffee mugs back into the shop Ellen arrived with the bacon baps and dropped the bag on the desk. He perched on a high red stool and opened the bag.

She grabbed a bottle of brown ketchup from the kitchen cupboard and squeezed a long dollop onto the bacon rashers then squashed the bread roll back together again and took a large bite. 'Ooh, that's sooo good,' she said licking the ketchup from her lips.

She looked like a ten-year-old, Mark thought biting into his bap then fondly shook his head.

'So, who else was at this taste panel?' she asked.

Mark described Olga, Margaret, Jason, and Ayesha.

'And at next week's session we'll be tasting jam doughnuts. So, I'll probably use the vouchers to kick-start my healthy diet regime.'

Finishing the last mouthful of her bap, she nodded. 'And who was running the group? Was it a woman, like a home economics' teacher?'

'No,' he said wistfully thinking of Sarah. 'She is what's called a sensory analyst, and her name is Sarah, and she's nice.'

Ellen raised an eyebrow. 'Oooh, and how old is she?'

He shuffled uneasily on the stool. 'Em, I think she said she was thirty-six.'

'Married? Living with someone? Children?' she asked jumping down from her stool.

'Ellen,' he said and sighed. 'I've absolutely no idea'

Mark drained his coffee. He didn't want to make more of it than it was because he knew if Ellen found out that he liked Sarah she'd start the same tirade again. She would bombard him with questions for months.

He knew she was right, and it was high time he built up a social life but found the whole idea, especially dating, such a daunting prospect. Therefore, in a positive step towards making new friends he'd decided to go along to the taste panel and had also joined a reading group at the library.

She crossed over to the side of the shop and began tidying the shelf with paint brushes and paints. 'Hopeless!' She exclaimed. 'You're absolutely hopeless. Why didn't you ask all the important questions, like if she is a free and available?'

He scrunched the empty bag in his hands and getting down from the stool tossed it into the bin. She was right of course, but he felt so out of practise with it all. 'I know,' he said. 'Maybe I'll find out next week.'

Looking up, she grinned. 'Yeah, we'll have a few practise sessions before next Thursday.'

He moaned and pulled a face at her, and she giggled. She was like a daughter to him now and when he'd first found out how dreadful her childhood had been it had made his stomach clench. How could any parents neglect and not want to care for such a lovely little girl was beyond his powers of reasoning.

She studied a painting lying on the work bench that she wanted to frame, and he stared at the curls on the top of her head. Maybe if Jessie hadn't miscarried their baby girl she might have turned out like Ellen. He felt an ache of loneliness lodge in his chest.

Later, while he was working in the dark area with a black & white photograph of the Ponte Vecchio Bridge in Florence, Ellen popped her head around the door to tell him he had a visitor.

Rebecca, dressed in a brown trouser suit with a camel wool coat draped over her arm stood near the cash desk.

'Hello,' she said smiling at him. 'Thought I'd just drop by to say hello and drag you out for a quick bite to eat. That's if you haven't already had lunch?'

He was dumbfounded. 'W…well, no I haven't.'

Ellen interrupted. 'Wow, what a stroke of luck. Mark was just saying how he'd nip out soon and try the new café on the high street. I've heard they do a lovely Panini?'

Mark turned to scowl at Ellen, but Rebecca raved. 'Yes, I've heard that too and that the salads are simply to-die-for.'

He looked between them and decided quickly that it would be rude to refuse Rebecca and the earbashing he would get from Ellen didn't bear thinking about.

'Love to,' he said smiling at Rebecca. 'I'll just get my jacket.'

***

Wishing he hadn't worn his old, but comfortable suede jacket that morning he walked beside her down the high street matching her long strides. She walked with an air of consequence with her head held high and shoulders pulled back. The self-important expression which played around her full lips made him feel a little unsure of himself.

She chatted about her busy morning in the office and how she'd longed to escape out for an hour into the autumn sunshine, and his mind raced. He was shocked that she had sought him out after their first meeting the night before. And if he was totally honest, just a little bit flattered.

Settling themselves at a table they both ordered Panini with rocket salad and sun-dried tomatoes. The conversation turned to Italy and the escorted tour she had booked. He relaxed back into the chair and decided to enjoy the experience. He'd simply, go with the flow, as Ellen often told him.

He told Rebecca about the trip to Venice and Rome that he and Jessie had taken before she was ill and his love of the

Italian artists. 'I could show you my paintings of St. Marks and the Doge Palace when we get back to the shop?' he offered. 'It'll give you a flavour for the place.'

'Hey, that'll be great,' she said fluttering her black eyelashes. Her eye lids were covered in a dark brown eyeshadow and the thick black eyeliner made them look harsh in the sun that flooded through the window. He wondered what her eyes would look like without the heavy make-up.

The conversation flowed easily between them, and he warmed to her deciding she wasn't as scary as he first thought. By the time they'd finished eating he'd formed a different opinion altogether from the night before.

She told him how she was raised in Preston Village but had moved to Preston Road when she got married. While she talked about her ex-husband and how awkward he'd been about their divorce, Mark thought she seemed full of confident bravado. At the same time, however, he could also sense her loneliness and vulnerability.

'He was a complete pain in the neck when I wanted to buy his share of the house,' she explained. 'But I've loved living there since the first day I set foot over the doorstep. And I don't really want to live anywhere else. I wasn't being snobby about it last night but that Olga woman irked me with her patronising manner.'

He smiled back and nodded. 'I know, but she may get better as the weeks go by?'

Rebecca smiled then started to look a little uneasy and fiddled with the napkin on the table. 'Well, now it's just little old me all alone in the house and going on holiday by myself.'

Mark knew this was a subject he could easily relate to, and they discussed the pros and cons of living alone and how difficult it was to start rebuilding a single life again.

'So, how did you feel when your wife died?'

'Em, w…well,' he muttered, wincing at the starkness of the question

Rebecca was an open book, but he couldn't talk about Jessie as she had done about her ex-husband. It felt too disloyal. He'd always been, and still was, wary with strangers until he got to know them. And even then, he knew he kept a lot buried inside. His mother had once called him, as deep as the ocean.

She must have realised how tactless she'd been and said, 'Oh, Mark, I'm sorry, I didn't mean it to come out like that!'

'It's okay,' he said. 'There's no harm done. Well, Jessie lived for eleven months after she'd been diagnosed with cancer. Much longer than what the doctors said she would. So, I had time to think about it and put plans into place.'

He hoped that was enough to say because he was still too embarrassed to tell anyone the stark truth about the week Jessie found out she had cancer. The call-back from the routine mammogram had come ten days after she'd told him she was in love with another man. She had been having an affair with him for six months and intended to move in with him. Within the next three weeks of body scans and waiting for test results they learned the cancer had spread throughout her body and the creep she'd been having an affair with had disappeared. Therefore, he'd had no other choice but to look after her.

Rebecca lowered her eyes and began to tear the paper napkin into little pieces. 'It's just that my mam is dying in a hospice and I'm sort of dreading the end because I don't know what to expect. My, father walked out on us when I was two and I can't remember anything about him. So, because I'm an only child it's going to be all down to me.'

He sighed knowing how lonely she must feel with no one to talk to and nodded. He knew exactly how it felt. Jessie had figured because she'd known him all her life that it was his duty as her husband, to look after her. She had never once admitted their marriage had been over years before the diagnosis and that it had been a sham. He knew Jessie had used him like a doormat but because she was dying, he'd felt defenceless.

Mark took her hand lying on the table and squeezed it. 'Are you close to your mam?'

'We were,' she said. 'Up until three months ago.'

'It's okay, you don't have to talk about it,' he said.

She smiled. 'No, I'm fine. I feel like I can talk to you because you've been through losing someone and must know how it feels to watch the person you love disintegrate in front of your eyes.'

'W…well, I,' he stuttered feeling out of his depth. Jessie and Sam had been his only family, so he had cared for her to the very end. Even Sam, to who she had never usually had a kind word, never left her bed side. He'd sat whimpering, tail flat on the carpet, and head bent looking at her with huge doleful eyes that had broken Mark's heart. After she'd died, he had grieved for her but not as a husband should. It had been more like a brother losing a sister because that is how their relationship had been at the end.

Rebecca said. 'Mam went into the hospice because she needed round the clock medication, and I couldn't keep up and work at the same time. The hospice is charity based and although there is no charge for the services, mam wants to make a donation. So, she asked me to look for assets to use and when I was sifting through all the paperwork, I found some documents form an adoption agency.'

'Oh, really?' Mark couldn't help being interested although he could see she was upset.

Her eyes filled with tears. 'Yeah, it turns out I was adopted when I was three months old, and I've started the process of trying to trace my birth mother.'

Mark was shocked. 'But this must be terrible for you!'

'It was and still is really,' she said. 'The last time I went to the hospice I just stared at her and felt so resentful that I couldn't speak a word. She's never told me about this for over forty years. She doesn't know that I know, therefore, she is more than happy to go to her maker without even telling me about it. And that, I just cannot forgive.'

Mark took a deep breath. 'Well, I'm not sure if this will help or not but it's extremely hard to manage secrets about someone that has died or is dying,' he said. 'Jessie's sister, Paula, knows nothing about the marriage problems we had. And, when she comes to see me, I always have Jessie's photograph on the fireplace. I sit patiently listening to how perfect and beautiful her sister was in every way. Paula makes caustic digs at me about how I failed her as a husband and how I'd always been more interested in my painting than poor Jessie. And she goes on and on until I want to scream at the unfairness at it all. But I don't think it's my place to spoil her memories, so I sit and take it on the chin and then as soon as she leaves, I put the photograph back in the drawer out of sight.'

Rebecca nodded and sniffed. 'Thanks Mark, it does help to talk. When I was little, I used to ask her why I didn't have any brothers or sisters and she'd say that they didn't want any more children and that I was more than enough. But now I know the actual truth and that she couldn't have any in the first place. Well, it sticks in my throat.'

Two big tears escaped from her eyes and Mark rubbed the back of her hand. 'Look, let's get out of here and walk back through the park.'

He could see the relief on her face while she gathered her bag and coat and he guided her through the door with his hand on her back. The air was cold but refreshing and he breathed in deeply. They walked a few steps then crossed over the road to the park and she swung her handbag while looking up at the leaves on the trees.

He was going to make a comment about the beauty of the orange, tan and red autumn colours then bit his lip with indecision. It might seem insensitive in a situation like this.

She said, 'The autumn colours are lovely, aren't they?'

He took her arm and pulled it comfortingly through his own as they walked. 'I was just going to say the same thing myself but then decided it might sound crass after what we've just been talking about.'

She smiled up at him. 'I could use a bit of ordinary right now. I'm afraid I've been far too heavy and unburdened myself onto you when we hardly know each other. I do tend to scare men away on first dates. I think I'm too forthright but maybe that's because of my job.'

'You're fine,' he said. 'It's not a problem.'

He liked the feel of her arm in his and because they were the same height they walked at a similar pace. He was more than happy to be in the park with this extremely attractive woman on his arm. What was just supposed to be grabbing a quick bite had turned into a lunch date and he smiled. It had made him relax in a woman's company without the pressure of the first date scenario. She smiled at him, and he squeezed her arm feeling he was walking forward into new beginnings, and for that, he was grateful.

All too soon he realised they were back in front of his shop. They swapped business cards and Rebecca suggested going for a drink on Thursday night after the next taste panel. He felt quite giddy with the excitement of another date.

He beamed and nodded while she touched his arm and pecked him briefly on the cheek. Turning to wave as she headed off down the road he wondered if the kiss was special. Or did everyone kiss cheeks after a daytime date. Maybe if it had been an evening date, he would have been expected to kiss her properly on the lips? Opening the shop door, he felt quite euphoric about the success of his impromptu lunch.

***

Fortunately, Ellen was serving a customer when he hung his jacket up which gave him minutes to compose himself and wipe the idiotic grin from his face.

But as soon as the customer left, she rounded on him. 'So, is that Sarah?' She asked. 'The woman who ran the taste panel last night.'

He raised an eyebrow and then realised the confusion. 'Oh, no,' he said. 'That's not her. That was Rebecca, she is one of the panellists, like me. She's going to Italy for the first time on holiday and is going to use her vouchers to try some new pasta dishes.'

Ellen whistled through her teeth like a boy. 'Wow!' she said grinning. 'Two women in one night? Way to go, Pop's.'

Chapter Three – Thursday 25th October

On Thursday morning Sarah crunched into a piece of toast and walked to the window in her lounge which overlooked The River Tyne and across to South Shields. She loved the fantastic views, and it was the main reason she'd bought the new-build, town house. Her mother had wanted her to buy somewhere in Preston Village where she had grown up and where the family still lived but she had been adamant.

'No, Mam,' she'd said. 'That's not going to happen. I am moving back to the area but I'm not settling back into life the way it was fifteen years ago. It has to be a fresh start.'

Her mam had pouted. 'But you can still have a fresh start in one of the terraced houses in the village where you know everyone,' she'd said. 'They're much cheaper and smaller. What on earth does a single girl need three bedrooms for?'

Her sister, Holly, had chipped in. 'Oh, she wants to swank about in her new pad throwing all the money around she's made in London!'

Sarah had silently counted to ten. 'No, Holly, I don't. And I wouldn't know how to swank. When Paul left me, his father bought my share of the flat because he wanted to keep it as an investment,' she said. 'So, I'm doing the same and investing my money into this property it makes more sense these days. And I don't like old houses. It's nothing personal they just don't suit me. I wouldn't have lived in an old property in London, so I don't want to live in one here.'

Holly had huffed and flounced out of the room while her mam made excuses for her. But Sarah knew Holly was jealous of her lifestyle and always had been. When Sarah had gone to university Holly had married the boy next door and was content to have her babies and follow in mams footsteps and that was great. But it hadn't been enough for her; she'd wanted a profession and a career.

Walking back into the bedroom to dress for work she chose a pale blue shirt to wear with her navy-blue suit. She looked in the full-length mirror and remembered how Paul had loved to see her in blue. He'd said it brought out the colour of her eyes. Swallowing hard she fought back the tears. Thinking of him was getting less and less but there was still sometimes it crept up on her. Memories from her previous happy life could fill her mind with simply the sound of a CD, mention of a film, or programs they'd loved to watch on TV.

Turning from side to side she looked at her profile in the fitted suit and was glad to see she looked a slim size twelve. It was a good day. On bad days she often thought she looked a chubby size fourteen.

She'd had a weight problem and had been fat all her childhood up until she turned sixteen then with the help of her friend, Christine, she had lost the excess. School days had been a bullying misery but when she had started university in size twelve jeans the relief of being accepted and fitting in with the crowd had been well worth all the effort.

She now went to the gym three or four times a week which she knew kept her weight in check because she would always have the type of body that gained weight easily. Folding her blue stripy shirt, she put it into her gym bag and pushed all thoughts of Paul firmly out of her mind. When she was working late to do the evening taste panels, she would usually keep the same shirt on all day but this evening she wanted to change and freshen up first.

***

'And why are you changing shirts tonight?' Christine asked when they met for lunch in the pub. 'Is it for this guy, Mark you were telling me about on the phone.'

Sarah looked at her oldest and dearest friend. Even after she'd moved down to London, they'd always stayed close. When Sarah was deciding whether to accept the promotion and move back to the Northeast Christine had pleaded with her to come home via texts, calls, and emails.

'No, not really,' Sarah said grinning. 'But I always think there's no harm in looking ones best.'

Christine dressed like an old hippie and was an inch from six foot in her stocking feet. She had black frizzy hair, protruding grey eyes that often looked as if they were standing out on stalks, and was very thin.

Sighing heavily, Christine reached across for Sarah's hand. 'Just be careful, honey,' she said. 'It's only these last two months that you've started to get over Paul. I couldn't bear to see you in an emotional heap again.'

Sarah knew it made sense. She'd been absolutely devastated when Paul left, and it had taken medication from her doctor, counselling, and the support from her family and Christine before she had clawed her way back to normality again. 'You're right. It's probably far too soon but he does have the loveliest smile,' she said dreamily.

'Well, why didn't you say?' Christine giggled. 'A cute smile gets me every time.'

Planning to have dinner in Tynemouth on Friday night they left each other, and Sarah hurried back to the office to get through as much work as possible before six o'clock.

**

The taste panel room walls were painted a drab cream colour and apart from the long wood table in the middle and the black plastic chairs the room was devoid of anything else.

There was no cooking at this session, but she set out the numbered plates, paperwork, water jugs and glasses ready for the panel. The thought of seeing Mark gave her butterflies in her stomach. She'd found it hard to concentrate all afternoon which she knew was silly. Other than their brief eye-to-eye contact, he hadn't given her any signs that he was remotely interested. But she was really looking forward to seeing him again.

While she emptied packets of jam and iced doughnuts in the kitchen, she saw Olga & Margaret arriving together and called out a greeting. They both answered in unison. She wondered if they were friends and hung out together? But then decided this was unlikely because they seemed what her mam would call, poles apart.

Her fingers were sticky with traces of sugar, and she fought the urge to lick at the sweetness wiping them with a cloth instead. Memories of her youth and when she'd been overweight flashed into mind and how on occasions, she could stuff herself with two or three cakes at a time. She shuddered at the memory.

Sarah heard Rebecca calling hello and carried the plates with jam doughnuts through to the room. Rebecca looked stunning in a short black skirt above her knee with thick black tights and knee-length black boots. A red roll-neck sweater completed her outfit, and her long hair flowed loose around her shoulders. It's no wonder Mark was smitten, she thought and glanced down at her boring, tailored work suit. She felt like what her mam would call, the poor relation.

'Hey, Sarah,' Rebecca said. 'Have you tried the new café on Queen Alexander's Road?'

Sarah placed the plates down the centre of the table. 'No,' she said. 'But my friend Christine has been and gave it glowing reports.'

'Well, she's right,' Rebecca said. 'The sandwiches and salads are simply to die-for. Mark and I called there for lunch last week and we were well-impressed.'

Sarah felt her stomach crash down to her court shoes. So, they are seeing each other, she thought. She sighed and felt her chest tighten. She knew she was being stupid, and Christine was right, she must have been mad to even think about another man. It was far too soon.

Margaret cried, 'Oh, my. And have we a little romance starting up between you two lovelies?'

Olga, dressed in a matronly grey twin-set and thick tartan skirt tutted with dismay at Margaret's silly comment just as Ayesha followed closely by Jason arrived and they all took their seats.

Sarah had removed the name cards this week and told them to sit anywhere but noticed Rebecca kept her handbag on the chair next to her. Obviously, this seat was meant for Mark.

He rushed through the door full of apologies. Rebecca patted the seat next to her removing her bag while he grinned and sat down. They did look good together Sarah decided, with Mark wearing black jeans, a grey jumper and black leather shoes.

Pushing the disappointment and Mark firmly from her mind, she began the session. 'So, I hope you all had a good week and I'm glad to see you've come back again. Panels always work best with at least six people,' she said. 'Now, the forms are the same as last week and we should have time to taste the six varieties of jam doughnuts then repeat the same with the iced.'

There was a general hub of excitement amongst everyone while Sarah put three jam doughnuts onto each of the six numbered plates and cut them in half. 'Also, just a little tip for this week. I've halved the doughnuts, but you might only want to take a small mouthful of each because if you eat the whole piece, you'll end up eating six doughnuts by the end of the session. And that might be a bit too much even for those of you with a sweet tooth!'

Olga grunted. 'Do you know, I don't think I've ever eaten a jam doughnut before. Are they a modern invention?' She asked fingering the string of pearls around her neck.

'Well,' Sarah replied. 'They're not traditional and I think historically they're American.'

Margaret gushed, 'Oh, I didn't know they were from America, but I have tried them before at the women's institute coffee morning. And they were lovely.'

'Hmph! American!' Olga exclaimed. 'And why are we not tasting products made in England?'

Sarah took a deep breath. This woman was certainly going to be a challenge for the next nine weeks, she thought, and was about to explain that she didn't choose what they tasted each week when Jason sat forward and intervened.

'No, Olga,' Jason said. 'These were not made in the USA. They are made here and are typically English now. Sarah meant the idea originated from across the pond.'

Sarah gave him a smile of thanks while a general discussion took place about how they were made, and Jason explained to the older ladies what he meant by the saying, across the pond.

Sarah pushed on. 'So, I'd be pleased if you could pay particular attention to the texture column on your forms this week,' she said. 'The lightness of the baked dough is especially important, and we can discuss this later. There may be some that are lighter than others.'

Silence descended when they all began trying the jam doughnuts and marking the forms while she sat back in her chair and looked around the group. Trying not to look or think about Mark and Rebecca she purposively focused her attention to the people sitting at the top end of the table.

Jason and Ayesha seemed very friendly together and she'd noticed how, although there was a choice of seats this week, they'd still sat next to each other. Ayesha looked just as beautiful today in an emerald, green tunic and Sarah loved the big silver earrings she wore.

Jason however, looked tired and she'd previously heard him telling Margaret the twins had been awake half of the night teething. Jason and Ayesha were an odd pairing, she thought, hearing them whispering together. Even though she strained her ears she was sure they weren't talking about the doughnuts. At one stage she heard Ayesha say the word marriage and something about Boxing Day.

Mark seemed to be finished first and laid his pencil down on top of the form then tried to catch her eye with a cute smile. Sarah knew she needed to get this association back onto a professional footing and smiled formally at him. It was her normal smile that she used for everyone and although she made sure it wasn't tight-lipped, she did feel a small amount of satisfaction when he shrugged and put his head down.

Clearing the plates and collecting the forms she repeated the same routine but with the iced doughnuts and while they all began tasting again, she quickly collated the jam doughnut results.

Margaret looked as if she was thoroughly enjoying herself and even Olga seemed absorbed in the pieces of doughnuts while she went from one sample to another marking different comments on her sheet. Rebecca tasted the smallest piece of each sample and her eyes never left Mark while leaning towards him at every opportunity.

He looked pleased with her attentions and commented about the tiny mouthfuls she had taken.

'Oh, I couldn't possibly eat six doughnuts all at once, I'd put on too much weight,' she said and giggled. She patted his hand in what Sarah thought a playful manner.

Sarah gathered the forms together and tried not to look at them.

Mark said, 'And how about you, Sarah. Do you never have the urge to taste any of these lovely doughnuts and tarts we've been eating?'

Startled, she tried not to look into his eyes. 'No, but I do taste them all in our department panels with the buyers and marketing teams. However, when we taste food, we don't swallow but spit it out into a pot.'

Margaret said, 'Oh, like the tea tasters do?'

Sarah smiled at her. 'Exactly,' she said.

Olga said, 'You, young people. You're all obsessed with slimming and diets. There's nothing wrong with a normal balanced diet and you won't put weight on that way.'

Margaret nodded. 'Olga's right,' she said. 'And in these chilly winter months you all need a hot meal instead of picking at those salad pots that I see everyone eating.'

Sarah smiled back at the ladies then quickly brought the group back together and discussed the results. There were discrepancies with the jam doughnuts and only Olga had chosen a sample that she thought had a better texture.

When Sarah explained this Olga insisted upon trying the samples again and Sarah braced herself for another confrontation. However, she was pleasantly surprised when Olga changed her mind, admitted she'd been mistaken and agreed with the others.

The iced samples had a definite best and better result, and a specific poor and worst result which everyone agreed to unreservedly. Sarah thanked them all and told them the results corresponded with her departments and that the management would be delighted with the scores.

Sarah put the vouchers on the table again and a discussion broke out about who had spent last week's vouchers and who was saving them for another time. She could tell Rebecca was itching to get away by pulling on her jacket and smiling at Mark who appeared to be just as keen. They were the first to pick the vouchers up and scuttle out of the room.

Sarah slumped back on her chair and gathered her forms together. Jason and Ayesha followed Olga out of the door and Margaret was last to leave but stopped and stood in front of her.

'Are you all right, my lovely?' she asked. 'You don't look as bright and breezy as last week?'

Sarah smiled at Margaret's home-knitted green jumper which was like one her mam wore. She stood up and started to clear the rubbish into a black bag. 'Oh yes, I'm fine, maybe just a little tired,' she said then felt her cheeks flush.

Margaret stroked the side of Sarah's arm. 'Don't let Olga wear you down,' she said. 'She's not an easy character to get along with but she means well. She just goes about things the wrong way sometimes.'

Sarah smiled. 'I was surprised when she admitted she was wrong. I thought I was going to have another battle on my hands.'

Margaret said, 'One thing I will say about her is that she's as honest as the days long. And I should know, I've known her since we were kids at school. But I'm the first to admit she can be a handful at times, in fact, that's why I stopped working for her.'

Sarah gasped. 'You worked for her?'

'Well, yes, I was her cleaner for years, but I finished last year. It was getting too much for me, but the truth was there's only so much a person can take. I called her Hyacinth Bouquet,' she said laughing. 'And even her husband, God rest his soul, was just like Richard in the sitcom, Keeping up Appearances. He travelled all over the country mainly to keep out of the house and from under feet!'

Sarah giggled at the comical expression on Margaret's face while she left the room. That explained a lot, she thought. They had been employer and employee in the past but that still didn't give Olga the right to demean Margaret in front of everyone.

She remembered her mam saying when she was little, that when you lived in a small town like Preston Village everyone knew each other in one way or another. And that, she decided, picking up her gym bag was another reason to be living up at Renaissance Point.

Chapter Four – Friday 26th October

Rebecca pulled into St. Oswald's hospice car park and parked her Mazda sports car. She looked across at the dual-level, purpose-built facility and then into the pretty courtyard surrounded with bushes, flowers, and trees. It was her mam's favourite place to sit on a nice day. But it was too cold for her today, she thought, and breathed a sigh of relief that the courtyard was empty.

This was good because it meant she could do the same as last time which was to reverse the car and leave. It also meant she could go without her mam knowing she'd arrived but couldn't bear to look at her.

She knew she was being ridiculous and juvenile, even pathetic, but simply couldn't stop herself. Every time she thought of her mam keeping the adoption a secret the feelings raged inside her chest into such anger that it frightened her. She was scared she'd lose control altogether.

She wanted to shout at her mam and demand, why, why, why, until she got satisfaction. But you couldn't do that in a quiet, serene place like this and she knew everyone would hate her for screaming at a dying woman.

Tears stung her eyes while she stared out of the windscreen, and she took deep breaths swallowing the lump of misery in the back of her throat. She still couldn't believe all this was happening and that the woman lying inside the hospice was not her mam. She wasn't related to her in any way and was a stranger.

Wiping the tears away with the back of her sleeve she had tried to remind herself that this woman who was dying had raised her as her own child for over forty years. And that she'd done it all on her own after her father had scarpered when she was little.

Rebecca knew it couldn't have been easy because she had worked all her life sometimes at two jobs to give her the chance of a decent education and lovely home. But no matter how much she tried to justify all of this it just didn't help.

The first few drops of rain hit the windscreen and she started the engine again, swung the car around and left the hospice grounds.

Driving back along the coast road towards home she remembered Marks words in the pub the night before. 'You know, Rebecca, you might regret not talking it through with her,' he'd said and patted her hand. 'Because there's one thing, I can say about death is that it is final, and you don't get any second chances once they've gone.'

Rebecca bristled with indignation at his disregard for what she'd told him when they had arrived in the pub. 'Thanks, Mark,' she'd said. 'And I know you mean well but I did say earlier that I didn't want to talk about it tonight.'

He'd looked a little dejected, but she'd pushed on with her original plan and behaved like she usually did on first dates. She had tossed her hair over her shoulders and smiled provocatively at him then spent the next hour being fun, flirty, and vivacious.

She'd thought it had gone well and that he was interested but noticed him pull away when she touched his arm or shoulder. Maybe, he was the type of guy who needed his own personal space, she'd thought. She had misread his body language altogether because he'd insisted upon leaving to go home and feed his dog. They'd walked to their cars in an awkward silence which had puzzled her, and she'd spent the rest of the night wondering why her plan hadn't worked. She didn't usually have these problems when she turned on her charm.

Pulling onto the gravel path and up to her front door she felt relieved that she hadn't gone into the hospice and picked up the bunch of flowers from the passenger seat.

She'd bought them to give to her mam but shrugged, maybe on another day she would feel stronger. She hurried through the large hallway and picked up post on route then headed into her office.

When her husband had moved out, she'd turned what should have been a fifth bedroom, into her office on the ground floor. She went straight to her desk now and slumped down into the chair.

Her slinky, white Persian cat, purred around her legs and she picked her up and snuggled her face into the soft fur while waiting for the laptop to connect. All she wanted was to feel as though she belonged somewhere and sighed. It was something she'd always taken for granted until she found the adoption papers. Now she felt it had been snatched away.

Scouring her emails from online dating sites she looked for new members or contacts from previous dates. She'd been a member on the sites since her divorce three years ago and sighed at the amount of money she had spent looking for another partner. At the beginning she hoped it would be money well spent when she was happily settled again with a new man.

The dates had been good and bad, but she always got a second date if she was interested in the man. Rebecca knew, not in a conceited way, that the men she didn't want to see again were all left wanting.

There were three emails waiting for a reply, but she carefully vetted each man's profile before deciding whether to answer. They had to fit into her criteria of what she classed as the possible husband number two. Mark fitted into her criteria nicely, she thought but after last night she wasn't too sure where their relationship was going. She remembered one of her grandpa's favourite sayings, never put all your eggs into one basket, and continued with her replies.

***

On Monday morning she arrived through the old doors of the law firm offices on Northumberland Square and bumped straight into one of the other associates, Greg Palmer.

'Rebecca!' He exclaimed. 'How are you doing? Good weekend?'

Oh no, Rebecca thought, this was the last person she wanted to see this morning but replied, 'Hey, Greg, nice to see you, I'm fine thanks.'

He put his hand on the open door which meant she would have to squeeze past him to enter the hall and she knew from past close encounters that this would not be a good idea.

He'd tried unsuccessfully over the last three years to get her embroiled in tight spaces and had made it blatantly obvious to everyone that he fancied her, but the feeling was not reciprocated.

'And how's that poor mam of yours doing?' he asked in a smarmy manner.

Greg was a widower, and in his mid-fifties, with a bald head, a huge, flabby belly which hung over his trousers suspended by braces. He had full, slavery lips, which if he'd been a woman, would have looked blown up with Botox.

The lips now looked wet, and a bubble of saliva sat in the corner of his mouth. Rebecca shuddered but answered, 'She was a little better at the weekend, thanks for asking.'

He ran a hand down the side of her arm, and she could feel the sweatiness of his palm through her silk blouse. 'Any time, he said. 'Anything at all, you only have to ask.'

If she'd thought for one minute that the query about her mam was genuine in the slightest, she would have been nicer to him, but she knew it was just a rouse. 'I really must push on, Greg, I'm running late.'

He stood aside to let her pass. 'Yes, yes, of course. Do you fancy grabbing a bite at lunch time?'

But she was through the doorway and hurrying into the main reception office shaking her head.

Susan, the secretary for all three associates sat at her desk in the centre of reception and grinned at Rebecca while she stopped to take post out of her pigeonhole. 'I see that Greg has just caught you?' she said and giggled.

'Oh, don't, Susan,' Rebecca said then tutted. 'It's awful first thing on a morning. He actually makes me want to heave.'

Susan burst out laughing. 'S…sorry, I didn't mean to laugh. It's just that he's so besotted with you, it's a bloody scream!'

Rebecca couldn't help smiling when she walked through to her office. 'Well, I'm pleased to give you entertainment value for the day, but I'm not interested,' she said. 'However, I would love a coffee and a natter?'

Susan perched on the edge of Rebecca's leather lined desk while they both sipped hot coffee. Their officers were on the ground floor of an old building and the law firm was even older. Rebecca had worked for the company since she'd finished university and had started as the junior working her way up through the old-boy ranks until she had hit the dizzy heights of an associate partner. She looked around the dreary worn-out room and shivered. Thankfully, most of her working week was now spent at home.

She did miss Susan however and gazed at her thoughtfully. Susan had been a great friend to her since the first day when she'd shown her the ropes, given her the background and history of the firm, and warned her about which men to avoid. And because all the other employees were male at the time, they'd bonded together from the start.

Rebecca told her about the taste panel sessions and described Mark and how she liked him.

'Well, I was more than surprised that you would go along to something like that,' Susan said. 'I wouldn't have thought it was quite your thing?'

Rebecca sighed and looked at her framed qualification certificates hanging on the wall above the well-worn chesterfield settee. 'It's not, really. But I saw it advertised and you get a £25 voucher for going, and well, you know me, I love to think I'm getting something for nothing. It was the way I was brought up. Thrift, thrift, thrift. And even though I am on a good salary now it's still a hard habit to break…' she paused for breath then quietly said, 'I'm always at a bit of a loss on a Thursday night now.'

Susan sighed. 'Of course, you used to go to your mam's house for dinner on a Thursday. It must be hard getting used to her not being around like she was.'

Rebecca hadn't told anyone at work about the adoption because she liked to keep up a professional stance and reputation. She'd learnt in the law business that as a woman, even if you were excellent at your job, you had to fight harder than any man would to stay on top.

Suddenly, she felt exhausted with the situation tumbling around in her mind and couldn't hold it inside any longer. She burst into tears and the floodgates opened.

Susan being a chubby woman with an ample chest, slid from the desk and threw both her arms around Rebecca while she sobbed as though she would never stop. Eventually the crying eased and after cuddles of reassurance from Susan, she felt calm enough to explain about the adoption.

'So far, I've got my birth certificate from the adoption agency and have registered my interest to contact my birth mother on the Adoption Contact Register. But it will depend on whether she wants to contact me and if she has what is called a qualified veto. If she has an absolute veto, then I won't be able to contact her, and I'll never be able to trace my real father.'

Susan smiled with eyes full of concern. 'And of course, you were only little when your father left?'

Rebecca wiped her face with a handful of tissues and then blew her nose. 'My, mam, well the woman dying in the hospice, only ever told me that my father ran out on us when I was two. But as it turns out he wasn't my real father anyway, so it doesn't matter,' she said and shrugged her shoulders.

Susan tutted. 'Rebecca, the woman dying in the hospice is your mam,' she said putting her arm along her shoulder. 'She's the one who brought you up and loved you.'

Rebecca nodded. She'd said this to herself a hundred times but now hearing confirmation from another person it sounded more real. 'D…do you really think so?'

Susan pulled her shoulders back and nodded. 'Well, I knew your mother years ago and although she was older than me, I know she didn't have an easy time. It would have been better if your dad had died because it would have been less of a scandal.'

Rebecca remembered Susan had been brought up in Preston Village and knew first-hand the downside of living in a small town. The gossipmongers must have had a great time.

'But who am I?' Rebecca asked. 'Where have I come from? And when mam dies where will I belong?'

She looked down at her black high-heels and felt her cheeks burn with embarrassment. 'I've been horrible and can't bring myself to go into the hospice to see her,' she said. 'I just cannot forgive the fact that she's never told me!'

Susan pondered. 'And your mam asked you to go through the paperwork to find some monies or assets?'

Rebecca nodded and looked at Susan's face. It was obvious her friend was mulling something over. 'What!' Rebecca almost shouted at her. 'What are you thinking?'

'Well, if your mam didn't want you to find the adoption papers, she wouldn't have given you permission to go through her stuff, would she?' Susan said. 'And maybe, if she didn't have the courage to tell you, she might be hoping you would find out for yourself.'

Rebecca jumped up from her chair and started to pace around the room. She thought about Susan's suggestion in a rational manner as if it was a work problem. Her mam had told her where the boxes were in the loft and that her insurance policies were kept in an old cake tin. And of course, that's where she'd found the adoption certificate. Susan was right, she thought, her mam had meant her to find out after all.

'Thanks, Susan, I owe you one,' she said grabbing her coat and bag then ran from the room hoping the staff in the hospice would allow her to visit without notice.

Chapter Five – Thursday 1ˢᵗ November
Sarah hurried from her office along the corridor and
upstairs to the taste panel room. She'd had such a busy day
and at one stage had worried she wasn't going to be there
for six o'clock. Today's session was party cocktail sausages
and mini scotch eggs. However, all the samples hadn't
arrived and knowing she wouldn't get a fair result without
the required amount she'd decided to leave off scotch eggs
from this panel.

Rushing into the room she flicked the lights on and flew
through to the kitchen to pre-heat the ovens. Deciding her
full bladder wouldn't last another hour she ran back out
onto the corridor and into the ladies.

Sitting in a cubicle she heard two familiar voices enter and
she glanced under the door recognising Margaret's brown
flat lace-up shoes.

She heard Margaret say, 'Oh, honey, what on earths the
matter, you look dreadful!'

She recognised Ayesha's voice and heard her burst into
tears then start to sob. Glancing under the door again she
saw Ayesha's felt slipper-shoes step towards Margaret and
Sarah knew the older lady was cuddling her.

Feeling in an awkward predicament Sarah didn't know
whether to flush and walk out of the cubicle and get
involved in the situation. She decided this might embarrass
Ayesha even more, so she stayed in the cubicle and waited
until they left. Looking at her watch she knew she would
still have time because the sausages only took ten minutes
to re-heat.

'I…I hate him, Margaret,' Ayesha sobbed. 'He's my
father, and I shouldn't say that but he's ruining my life and
I don't know what to do!'

Margaret soothed. 'There, there,' she said. 'It'll be all
right, he can't force you to marry this man, can he?'

Ayesha blew her nose. 'You don't understand. But I do thank you for trying,' she said. 'You see, that's exactly what he can and will do. It's what is called an arranged marriage and I have no choice in the matter.'

'Oh, Dear!' Margaret exclaimed. 'What a to-do!'

'Sorry, I shouldn't be burdening you with all of this because we hardly know each other,' Ayesha said. 'You just caught me off guard in the corridor.'

Sarah could imagine Margaret's concerned face when she said. 'Come-on let's get you a nice cup of tea with some sugar in it. That's always good when you're upset and I'm sure Sarah won't mind.'

They left the toilets and Sarah crept out of the cubicle feeling dreadful as though she'd been eavesdropping, but it certainly hadn't been intentional. Hurrying into the kitchen minutes later she cheerfully greeted Margaret and Ayesha while they were making tea.

'I hope you don't mind us making a cuppa?' Margaret asked, 'I've not had time for one and I'm gasping.'

Sarah looked at Ayesha's blotchy tear-stained face. 'No, of course not. Help yourselves. In fact, why not put seven cups out and we'll all have one.'

Margaret winked kindly at Sarah when Ayesha walked slowly back into the panel room and took her usual seat.

'Thanks honey,' Margaret said. 'She's got herself upset about something at home and I thought a hot cup of tea would help.'

Sarah began opening the packets of sausages and numbering her plates while Margaret carried the cups through. Mark arrived and insisted upon carrying the large catering tea pot for them.

Sarah joined them just as Rebecca breezed into the room. She heard Mark asking how her mam was doing and whether she'd had a busy week. Sarah was puzzled. Had he not heard from her since last Thursday or been out with her again? And, if they hadn't, she wondered why?

When she'd met Christine for dinner in Tynemouth on Friday night, she had told her about the disappointment at last week's session and how stupid she felt for dreaming up a fantasy about Mark. Christine had sympathised suggesting that maybe he wasn't so cute after all and maybe his gorgeous smile was just a fluke. To which Sarah had agreed and resolved not to think about him anymore.

Olga and Jason arrived and poured tea into their cups. Sarah sipped her tea and looked around the table at everyone. The group synergy was much better now that they'd all got to know one another and considering they were such a varied group this was surprising in such a short space of time. Sometimes panellists didn't start interacting until session six or seven.

Margaret had sat on the other side to Ayesha and every now and then she patted her hand in comfort while she drank her tea. Jason sat on the other side to Ayesha and looked at Margaret's actions with a puzzled look on his face.

This of course meant that Olga had sat next to Mark.

Olga turned to him and moaned. 'Blooming Halloween! What a carry-on last night,' she said. 'There must have been over ten groups of children banging on my front door. I was heartily sick of getting up and down to them. Trick or treat, they were all shouting which drives me crazy!'

Margaret protested in her gentle voice, 'Oh Olga, they are just having a bit of fun. I love to see them all dressed up and their little faces laughing. I always have bags of sweets to give them.'

'Sweets! Are you mad? No wonder you never have any money,' Olga retorted.

Mark and Ayesha smiled at Margaret. Sarah could almost feel the old lady's loneliness sitting at home on her own.

In his light-heartedly manner, Jason said. 'Well, when my girls grow up, I'll send them to your house first, Margaret.'

Olga wrinkled her nose and pulled back her shoulders. 'Where are their parents, that's what I'd like to know? Fancy leaving them to roam the streets in the dark and the same ones will be shouting on the TV if they're abducted by one of these paedophiles!'

Sarah saw Jason open his mouth to retaliate but she stopped him before an altercation broke out.

'Now,' she said. 'Our third session is party cocktail sausages, and we were also supposed to taste party Scotch eggs but not all my samples haven't turned up, which is annoying, to say the least. Therefore, this week's session won't run for as long as normal.'

While she put the sausages onto plates and placed them down the centre of the table the smell of cooked meat rose temptingly from the sausages. 'First, I'd like you all to cut the sausages in half and look at the texture. Ask yourselves, are there small pieces of meat in the mix or is it a smooth pulp texture. I'll tell you afterwards which sample has the highest meat content which is one of the attributes we pay great attention to when buying meat products. It is law now that every supplier in the country has to add this information to the label or sleeve.'

Everyone started to take the individual sausages from the plates while Sarah looked at Ayesha. She dressed in a plain black tracksuit today and wore only a scrap of make-up, although this didn't deter from her natural beauty. She did, however, look sad and tired. There were dark shadows under her eyes as though she hadn't slept for days. In fact, Sarah thought, it looked as though she had the whole world's problems resting on her young shoulders.

Sarah could tell she wasn't interested in the sausages this week while she fidgeted with her pencil. Usually, she listened intently to Sarah's instructions but obviously, the difference in sausage texture was a miniscule issue compared to her situation. Sarah couldn't begin to understand what it must feel like, especially at her age, to be married off to a stranger.

She wondered if Jason knew and was thinking the same thing himself because he kept watching her with concern out of the corner of his eye.

Everyone finished and they discussed the results within an hour of starting and when Sarah laid the vouchers out again, she saw Mark lean forward and look at everyone.

'I just wondered because we've finished early whether anyone wants to come to the pub for a quick drink?' he asked. 'Rebecca and I went to The Fox Hunters last week and it was a nice end to the evening.'

Sarah was shocked and dumbfounded especially by the look of surprise and hurt on Rebecca's face. And why, she wondered, if they were now an item would he want to invite other people along?

Olga thanked him but refused. Ayesha excused herself because her father would be expecting her at home. But Jason and Margaret agreed to join him and picked their vouchers up from the table. Sarah was in a quandary. Her gym class wouldn't start for another fifty minutes, and she was full of curiosity.

'Sarah?' Mark asked. 'Can we tempt you?'

She accepted giving him the first smile of the night.

***

They all trouped into the pub and found a corner table while Mark asked everyone what they wanted to drink and headed for the bar. There was a lively atmosphere in the large room with music playing in the background and people laughing enjoying their early evening drinks.

Rebecca's face looked thunderous, and Sarah could feel the woman's eyes boring into her back while she sat turned towards Jason.

'It's such a shame Ayesha hasn't come along,' Sarah said to him.

Jason told Sarah quietly about Ayesha's arranged marriage and how worried he was about her. 'I just think it's disgusting! Arranging and forcing young girls into marrying older men just because of their family connections. It's like being sold into slavery in the dark ages.'

Sarah sighed. 'I can't think of anything worse than being forced to live with someone you don't even like, let alone love.'

Jason's usual easy-going demeanour was full of genuine concern. 'I've read on the internet that the government also think it is abhorrent and simply wrong. They are trying to take decisive action to make it illegal but none of this will happen for a while,' he said sighing heavily and shaking his head. 'And that of course, is not going to help poor Ayesha, is it?'

While they quietly discussed the situation, she could see Margaret trying her best to make conversation with Rebecca. But she could also tell by the sneer on Rebecca's face that she thought Margaret a silly interfering old woman.

Mark arrived with the drinks on a tray and wouldn't under any circumstances accept the money. 'No, this one is on me,' he insisted. 'If we come again then someone else can buy the next round.'

Rebecca pounced upon him stroking his arm and giggling at every word he spoke while Margaret and Jason struck up the same conversation about Ayesha.

Mark sat forward to sip his drink and smiled at Sarah. 'So, do you live locally?' He asked. Rebecca leaned forward too obviously not wanting to be left out of the conversation.

His eyes were smiling directly at Sarah. She felt her mouth become dry and took a gulp of her drink. 'Oh, yes. I've just bought a town house up at Renaissance Point with the most fabulous views of the river,' she said. 'I absolutely love it.'

A discussion between everyone followed about the extensive regeneration program which had changed the redundant Albert Edward Docks. Sarah told everyone how amazed she'd been upon returning from London to see how much North Shields had changed with the new water park, outlet shopping centre, fish quay, and the new marina.

'Yeah, it certainly has,' Mark said. 'And I'm hoping next year to buy one of apartments on Quayside Court, just off Bell Street.'

Rebecca snapped to attention. 'Really, Mark, I wouldn't have thought you would like new-build properties. Personally, I couldn't think about leaving Preston and my beautiful old house,' she said and smiled playfully at him.

It looked to Sarah as though they shared secrets unbeknown to the rest of the group.

A group of men were standing at the bar and suddenly they all burst out laughing loudly. Everyone looked across to see where the loud noise was coming from, and Sarah glanced at Jason who made eye contact with one of the men. His whole face seemed to glow with pleasure. Hmm, she pondered, maybe he knew the chap at the bar but then scolded herself again about making more assumptions.

She diverted her gaze back towards Rebecca and Mark. Rebecca's face was right in front of Mark's nose, and she saw him visibly cringe. He certainly didn't look very comfortable sitting close to her.

This gave Sarah new hope that they weren't an item, and she couldn't help but feel her spirits rise. Finishing her orange juice, she remembered her resolution to stop thinking about him and said, 'Well, I'd better get going to my gym class.'

She pulled on her jacket and thanked Mark for the drink.

'Oh, I'll walk to the door with you,' Margaret said. 'And then nip to the loo. This lager Mark has so kindly bought is running straight through me.'

Sarah noticed the look of distain on Rebecca's face and then Jason's smile of fondness towards Margaret.

Mark put his hand on Margaret's arm. 'My, pleasure,' he said smiling. 'It's nice to get the chance to buy a young girl like you a drink.'

Margaret let out a giggle and gently touched the side of his cheek. 'You remind me of my oldest son,' she said. 'He was a right charmer, too.'

Everyone laughed and Sarah could tell the group sensed Margaret's loneliness and had taken her to their hearts.

When Sarah turned to leave the table, she said. 'And next week could everyone be prompt, please? I'll be in the room an hour earlier than usual to cook the turkey crowns. See you all then, goodnight.'

Margaret walked with Sarah towards the exit.

Suddenly, Margaret took hold of her hand and said, 'He's got a twinkle in his eye for you.'

Sarah stopped and looked at her. 'Excuse me,' she said. 'Who has?'

Margaret smiled. 'Well, Mark, of course. His eyes light up when he looks at you.'

'Aah, I think the lager has gone right to your head,' Sarah said laughing while she went out through the swing doors. But once outside on the pavement she couldn't stop grinning.

Chapter Six – Friday 2nd November

Ayesha made her way home after the taste panel with the same sick and unhappy feeling she'd had since the day her father had announced her marriage. She longed to have the freedom that her English friends were allowed to plan her own career, eat whatever food she liked, design her own clothes, and read any books that interested her.

Turning the corner onto Spring Terrace, she kicked at a stone as she walked along the pavement deep in thought. Perhaps the man they'd chosen would be okay and she was worrying unnecessarily? But whoever he was, he would not be her choice which was what upset her.

When she was fourteen, she'd found her first Mills and Boon novel at her friend, Becky's house and they'd devoured it together drooling over the hero. Since then, and because the books would be banned by her father, she had read them in secret and had formed the image of her ideal boyfriend.

He would be tall, good-looking, with broad shoulders, and strong. But at the same time, he would be protective although allowing her the freedom she craved. They would meet and fall in love naturally and have a family because they wanted children and not because she was forced into doing so. She was saving to buy herself a kindle to read new books in private without her father knowing anything about them.

Two girls she had known from school crossed the road and called out a greeting. Ayesha waved at them wondering if they appreciated how fortunate they were. When she stopped outside their corner shop, she thought about the friends she'd made at the taste panel and how she would have loved to join them in the pub. But because her parents didn't know where she went on a Thursday evening, and thought she was at Salsa dancing with Becky, she hadn't been able to think of another excuse.

She looked up at the windows above the shop which she'd known all her life as her home but felt it was more like a prison now. And when she thought of Boxing Day, she shivered knowing her life would change beyond all recognition.

Opening the front door to the shop she saw her mother behind the counter who called out a greeting. It was a typical square shaped room with shelves crammed full of things that people bought ad-hoc to avoid a trip to a supermarket. The long unsocial opening hours that her parents had always worked was the basis of its success and good profits.

'It'll be for you three when we are too old to run it,' her father would often chant as he puffed his chest out with pride. But she'd never been able to appreciate this because his next sentence was always, 'My sons will have careers here in the shop and my beautiful daughter will marry well and live for her husband. She'll give us many grandchildren to continue the family business.'

Her mother looked tired tonight but as serenely beautiful as ever. She told Ayesha about their busy day and how she longed to put her feet up with a cup of tea. Ayesha walked past her behind the counter and agreed to start dinner for the family.

The stairs to the big maisonette above the shop were in the back of the stock room and were scruffy with marks on the paintwork where boxes had been carried through to the front. The carpet was old, and thread-bear and she climbed each step wearily filled with dread at the conversation that would inevitably take place after dinner.

She'd decided to ask her father if he would at least postpone the wedding until next year. From what Jason had told her she would have more fighting power if the government kept their word and made it illegal or at least it would give her more time to plan.

When she got to the top of the stairs her two brothers were running between the lounge and bedrooms playing games and whooping with laughter. She watched them fondly and hoped they would make the most of their carefree childhoods because in years to come, they might feel as trapped and miserable as she was.

After dinner she got up from the long dining table, but her father instructed her to sit back down then told her brothers to clear the dishes and go to their room. She knew this was it and he was going to tell her about the man she had to marry. She folded her hands in her lap under the table and squeezed them tight. Her palms were sweating, and her heart began to race.

Her father took a photograph from the inside pocket of his long-jewelled tunic. He'd arrived back from a visit to his elder brother, Talin. After her grandparent's deaths in Deli last year, Talin was now traditionally head of the family. Ayesha knew according to the Hindu faith and Indian cultures he was responsible for important family decisions and rules. And the other family members had no choice but to abide by them. It was her Uncle Talin who had chosen the man, arranged the marriage, and helped her father negotiate her dowry with the family concerned.

He placed the photograph on the table in front of her and although she'd sat with her head bowed and her eyes closed, she knew she would have to open them now and look at her fiancé. She peeked at the photograph then gasped in shock. His face was small, and badly pock-marked with what she could only describe as thin, cruel lips. He wore gold rimmed glasses, had small brown eyes, and smudges of grey in the sides of his black hair.

She could feel her stomach heave and she swallowed hard. She managed to stammer, 'H…how old is he?'

'His name is Sachan, and he is thirty-one. He has an excellent job in banking, and you'll be happily settled for life with him, Ayesha.'

She dragged her eyes from the photograph and looked around the room at the dated striped wallpaper and dimly lit chandelier hanging from the ceiling. Taking a deep breath, she tried to find the right words to tell him how she felt but the panic inside her rose and she cried, 'But he's horrible! He's old and I can't do it. I just cannot touch this strange man.'

She looked wildly across at her mother for support, but she sat with her head and eyes cast downwards.

'What!' Her father roared and jumped up from the table. 'How dare you be so ungrateful? He's a great match for you and any other good Indian daughter would be on her knees thanking me and dreaming of her future happiness.'

He strode towards her, and she flinched back as though he was going to strike her. There was spittle in the corner of his mouth and his eyes were blazing with temper. She was terrified.

She started to sob, and he stood glaring down at her. Cowering under his glare she tried to say something, but her mouth was too dry, and her heartbeat pounded in her ears.

He lowered his face to within an inch of her eyes and she could smell his breath when he heaved in and out.

Slowly and deliberately, he said. 'You *will* marry Sachan. And, you *will* be the dutiful daughter I have raised. You *will not* bring shame on our family and *will* write a respectful letter to your uncle Talin thanking him for this match.'

He grabbed her wrist and the two yellow-gold bangles dug cruelly into her skin. She cried out in pain and for one split second she saw her mother raise her head. But when he dragged her from the chair and flung her across the room, she saw the terror etched on her mother's face who quickly lowered her gaze once more.

'Now, get to your bedroom and start praying to Allah to be forgiven,' he said and growled. Then picking the photograph up from the table he forced her hand open and pushed it into her palm.

Suddenly, he released her, and she stumbled back and out of the room. Blinded by tears streaming down her face she ran into her bedroom, closed the door, and flung herself onto the bed. She cried and cried until her throat felt raw and her head throbbed. How could he have been so horrible, she sobbed into her pillow. And although her parents had never been lovingly demonstrative, she had always thought they did love her.

Although now, she wasn't too sure. Her mother should have helped or at least tried to defend her but since Ayesha had reached her tenth birthday her mother had sided with her father's wishes. And of course, she too, feared him.

Ayesha had always thought of herself as more English than Indian and had spent her life feeling torn in two. She was a British citizen and used to English ways and although half of her wanted to be a dutiful daughter because she did love her family, the other half rebelled against it.

Drying her face, she got up, removed her sari, and pulled on pyjamas. All she could see ahead was cooking meals, sex with an older man which absolutely terrified her, and having babies for the rest of her life.

Lying awake she watched each hour of the clock tick by and tried to think of a way out of the situation, but her brain tumbled around in circles. If she stayed until Christmas, she would have to do exactly what her father wanted because she knew he wasn't bluffing and would indeed thrash her into subservience.

The other alternative was to run away but would she be brave enough to start a new life elsewhere on her own? And, if she did, it would mean never seeing her family again. But there again, if she stayed, she would be married and living with Sachan after Christmas.

She wondered if he was as strict and controlling as her father, or perish the thought, even worse? The image of his awful face was imprinted in her mind and the thought of him groping at her body made her wrap her arms around herself and tremble with fear.

After hours of fitful sleep her alarm clock buzzed, and she dressed for work in a plain black sari. It suited her mood. It was as if there'd been a death in the family. She was ignored at breakfast by both her parents and only her two brothers chattered to her in ignorance of the argument the night before.

***

While the boys left for school, and she set off down the road she wondered when they would be working in the shop alongside their parents. She'd had to do this from the age of twelve to sixteen and had hated every minute. However, when she left school with excellent exam grades and was accepted for the job at the medical centre with a good salary, her father had agreed to release her.

When she walked through the swing doors into the doctor's surgery her mood lifted when an old lady who she'd helped the day before greeted her with a big smile and a special thank you hug. Ayesha beamed with pleasure and then proudly joined her work colleagues behind the reception desk.

'Are you ill?' Becky asked. 'You look dreadful. And what's with the plain black sari, has somebody died?'

She tried to smile but her cheeks ached from crying the night before. 'No, I'm fine. It was just a sleepless night and a big argument with my father. I didn't feel like being jolly and colourful this morning.'

Becky put her arm along Ayesha's shoulder. 'Look, let's get on with the appointments now and when the dragon goes to the meeting, we'll have a coffee and try to sort something out,' she said and smiled.

Ayesha nodded. She knew Becky wouldn't understand because her English friends never could, but she was grateful for her kindness. She sighed then forcing a cheerful note into her voice she picked up the next telephone call.

The girls had nick-named the practice manager, Mrs Simpson, a dragon behind her back. But Ayesha thought the name unjust because from her first day the manager had been especially kind to her. At her yearly appraisal, Mrs Simpson had told her she was delighted with her high standards of work and that she was a valued member of the team. Ayesha's heart had soared with pride and happiness.

Being able to help people gave her such a buzz of satisfaction and she always ended her day feeling it had been worthwhile. The main reason however, that she loved working in the centre was because she was an equal and well respected for the job she did. Which was the total opposite to being at home. No matter how hard she worked there was no credit, it was just expected from her.

When she'd first left school she had dreamed of becoming a nurse or a doctor, but her father had forbidden this. She had begged him, 'But once I qualify the salary is excellent and it will help the family so much and mother could reduce her hours in the shop, in fact you both could stop working so hard. I'd like to help, father,' she'd said.

He'd chortled and patted her head. 'There's little point in doing all that training because you'll be married long before then and looked after by your new husband. You won't need a career. All you'll need to know is how to raise babies.'

At coffee time Ayesha told Becky about her new friends at the taste panel and how Jason had learned that a new law to make arranged marriages illegal could be brought in soon.

'Jason is like the older brother I wished I had to protect me. And Margaret is like the soft side of my mother. The way she was when I was little. It was lovely having a cuddle from her it made me feel so safe and warm.'

'Aah, that's nice,' Becky said. 'So, is that what the fight with your dad was about?'

Ayesha nodded her head and told Becky the whole story then showed her the photograph of Sachan.

Nineteen-year-old Becky wrinkled her pretty nose in distaste. 'But you can't marry him,' she said. 'He's an old man!'

Ayesha swallowed the lump in her throat. 'I know, he's horrible,' she mumbled.

'Don't worry,' Becky said hugging her. 'We'll do something to get you out of it.'

'I was thinking of running away,' she whispered looking over her shoulder as if her father would materialise at any minute. 'But I don't know if I'm more scared of doing that then staying and going through with the marriage.'

'But you can't leave. This is your job, and we all love you working here.'

Ayesha smiled and rubbed her arm. 'Well, either way I will be leaving because my father won't let me work when I'm married. I'll be producing babies from the first day I'm married,' she said. 'And, I'm dreading having to give Mrs Simpson my notice in December. Oh, Becky, what am I going to do!'

Chapter Seven – Thursday 8th November

Sarah had checked the cooking instructions on the pack labels for the turkey crowns and put them into the oven knowing she had an hour to wait. She'd brought her laptop to finish a comparison research project. This group of products were BBQ packs of chicken, burgers, and sausage to have in store for spring. The comparison between size, weight, appearance of packaging, price, and sensory attributes were important to the buyers and marketing managers. And Sarah took great pride in her contribution to the process.

A gentle tap made her look up to see Mark pop his head round the door.

'I'm early. Is it okay to come in, or do you need peace and quiet?' he asked with a big grin on his face.

A flush of happiness flooded through her. 'No, that's fine,' she said smiling. 'I've just put the turkey crowns into cook and I'm catching up on some paperwork.'

He walked into the room and stood facing her. 'Oh, right,' he said. 'I've had a lot on today and didn't have time to go home first, so I thought I'd come in and see what I could spend my vouchers on,' he said. 'But the store is packed, and I felt more in need of a coffee. Can I make you one?'

Sighing contentedly, she watched him turn towards the kitchen. 'I'd love one, white, no sugar, please.'

He wore a brown fisherman's sweater and brown corduroy trousers. A little dated, she thought, but couldn't help admiring his broad shoulders when he strode across the room. Sarah saved the spreadsheet knowing she wouldn't be able to concentrate and wished she'd made more of an effort dressing that morning. She fidgeted with her fringe and hoped her lips lip gloss was still in place. They chatted about the group and how well everyone was getting along together, and how nice it had been in the pub.

Carrying the coffee mugs, he sat down next to her. 'Hmm, I can smell the turkey cooking. It wouldn't be Christmas without it, would it?' He said, 'So, what are you doing for Christmas, do you and your partner stay home or travel?'

She tried to remember what she'd told him to give the impression she had a partner, or was he just probing to find out her circumstances?

At the risk of upsetting herself she decided upon the truth. 'Well, I'm on my own now. My, partner, Paul, left me six months ago. We'd lived together in London for nine years, but he met a woman who is a model in Milan and is living there now.'

She watched his grin fade and a look of empathy spread across his face.

'That's terrible,' he said and laid his hand on her arm.

She could tell the gesture was in genuine sympathy but still felt her skin tingle at his touch. It was the second time this reaction had surprised her but then she remembered Rebecca's delighted face when she'd talked about lunch with Mark.

Sarah decided that she would never go behind another woman's back and date her guy. Paul had cheated on her, and she knew how horrible it felt. She moved her arm to close the document on her laptop.

Until she knew for certain they weren't an item, she wasn't going to make a fool of herself again. 'Yeah, so I'm not really looking forward to it this year. Too many memories of Christmases past to haunt me,' she said but then lifted her voice. 'But my family are just down in the village, and I'll not be alone. Plus, my oldest friend, Christine, might come to stay.'

His hand stayed where she'd broke away from him and she looked down. They were large manly hands with hairs on the back of his fingers. The type of hands that could steady and support a woman, she thought. Not like Paul's young hands with perfectly manicured fingernails. But she'd had gotten used to Paul's hands, and after nine years had trusted them completely. When she found out that those same hands had betrayed her by touching another woman, her world had fallen apart.

Mark stared at her and she looked deep into his eyes. Were Mark's hands to be trusted, she wondered, and more to the point, when would she ever trust another man again?

He said quietly. 'It's not easy doing the first one. My first Christmas after Jessie died was horrendous, but I can honestly say it does get better.'

She shook herself and tore her eyes away from his. 'Oh, thanks, but I'll be fine,' she answered and lifted her chin. 'After all, it's the season to be jolly and it'll probably be nothing that a good bottle of wine can't shift.'

He looked a little hurt at the rebuff but as much as she liked him, she was determined to keep this relationship on a professional basis and nothing else. 'And what about you? Will you be spending Christmas with family?' she asked. 'Or with Rebecca?'

He raised an eyebrow. 'Rebecca?' he asked. 'Why on earth would I spend Christmas with Rebecca?'

Cursing herself for the rash remark she felt her cheeks burn. 'Oh, I just thought you two were dating or something. Margaret thought you were.'

He smiled. 'Aah, Margaret,' he said nodding. 'Now, I understand. No, we are not dating. Rebecca's mam is dying in a hospice and because I've been through it all with Jessie, I have been trying to help her. She is someone else who's going to have a tough Christmas.'

Suddenly, the door opened, and Rebecca breezed in. 'Oh, hello,' she said stiffly. 'I do hope I'm not interrupting anything?'

Sarah sprung up from her seat and away from Mark as if caught in the act of committing adultery.

Mark, however, didn't appear perturbed. 'Speak of the devil,' he said easily. 'I got here early too, and we were just talking about our Christmas plans while the turkey is cooking.'

Sarah excused herself to check the turkey crowns and scurried off into the kitchen. Margaret arrived next calling a cheery hello to them all and Sarah watched her plonk her old grey handbag onto the table.

While numbering the plates and looking through drawers for cutlery she listened to their conversation through the hatch.

Mark was chatting about the smell of the turkey cooking and Margaret began to regale them with stories and memories from Christmases when her two boys were little. 'Although I'd not had much to give them, I'll always treasure the memories,' she said. 'You see, my husband ran off when they were ten and six. I never knew why or where he'd gone and, in those days, there was no way of tracing people not like there is now on this tinternet.'

Rebecca giggled and Mark smiled while helping her remove her anorak. 'It's called the internet, you, silly goose,' he said and draped an arm along her shoulders.

Sarah watched Margaret soaking up the attention like a sponge. Poor woman, she thought sadly, she must have been apologising all her life since the day her husband left as if it was her fault.

Sarah went through and put the plates onto the table. 'It was a bit like that when I was little, Margaret,' she said. 'Mam and dad didn't have much to give us throughout the year, but we always had a good Christmas.'

Margaret turned her wedding ring around on her finger. 'T…thank you, she stuttered. 'Olga reckons I shouldn't wear my wedding ring, but I've just got so used to it being on my finger. And it's not as if I am divorced because I've never heard another word from him since that day. So, I don't know whether he's dead or alive, re-married, or what, really.'

Mark shook his head slowly. 'That's terrible,' he said gently. 'And have the boys ever tried to trace him?'

Sarah saw Margaret's gentle hazel eyes fill with sadness. 'Thank you all for your interest,' she said. 'I think my oldest son did try a few years ago but didn't get far and gave up. He's in Australia now and my youngest lives on The Isle of Man. So, I don't see a lot of them.'

Sarah could tell Margaret was getting flustered. She kept thanking them and her shoulders were drooped. She ran a hand through her thin, grey hair.

Sarah thought it best to change the subject, and said, 'Why don't you make us a pot of tea, Margaret?'

Her face brightened immediately. 'Oh yes, honey, I can do that nicely,' she said getting up and following her into the kitchen.

While Sarah checked the turkey temperatures Rebecca appeared at the hatch and asked Margaret if she could help carry the large tea pot. She gave her a smile of true sincerity.

While they worked together pouring milk into a jug, finding cups and a sugar bowl, Sarah heard Rebecca offer to help Margaret trace her husband.

'It wouldn't be through the firm,' Rebecca said. 'Therefore, there won't be a charge.'

And although Margaret thanked her repeatedly, in the end, she refused.

While pouring tea Margaret asked Mark, 'Do you have any children?'

Mark shook his head slowly. 'No, we never quite got there. We had a couple of miscarriages over the years which were desperately sad,' he said. 'Not being a father is my one big regret in life, Margaret.'

Rebecca took his hand and squeezed it. 'That's awful, darling,' she soothed. 'It's also my biggest regret too. My, husband and I tried for years when we were married and although the doctors gave us both a clean bill of health nothing happened. We tried IVF once, but I was so poorly with it we gave up.'

Margaret commiserated with them both. 'How tragic,' she said. 'Two lovely people like yourselves wanting babies and yet, there's all these young girls having them and can't afford to look after them properly, so they end up in care.'

Sarah set a sharp carving knife onto the table while everyone sipped their tea thoughtfully. The door opened and broke the melancholy mood. Jason and Ayesha arrived laughing together. More tea was poured, and Sarah noticed that Ayesha looked much brighter than the previous week.

Ayesha was wearing a fabulous cobalt blue and silver sari. Her Bindi was painted in the middle of her forehead and both her hands were patterned with henna. She told everyone how she'd been to a cousin's birthday party.

Rebecca and Margaret both raved over her sari when Sarah heard the timer buzz in the kitchen and hurried through to remove the turkey crowns. There was only Olga left to arrive, and just as Sarah thought how unusual it was for her to be late, she hurried through the door surrounded by the cloying smell of Chanel No.5.

'I didn't think I was going to get here today because I was waiting for the police to arrive,' Olga said unbuttoning her padded black jacket and sitting next to Mark.

Mark spun his head around towards Olga. 'Are you okay?'

Olga smiled at him. 'Oh yes, thank you. They called to see me about the complaints I've made about the yobs hanging around on our street. They've been such a nuisance this year with the blooming fireworks. On Bonfire night they were throwing bangers at my front door!'

Mark looked shocked. 'But that's terrible. Did you call the police when it was happening?' he asked. 'My, dog, Sam, was terrified this year. It seemed so much louder than previous years. The noise sounded like World War three was erupting!'

'Yes,' Olga said and snorted. 'Of course, they were too busy to come out on the 5th and turned up this afternoon to take a statement. They insinuated that it could have been my fault because I'd chased them from the street a few nights earlier. It's a disgrace! I think the whole night should be banned as well as the fireworks.'

Jason protested. 'But you can't say that. It's not fair to ruin a great night especially at organised firework displays just because of young idiots. Lots of people get a great deal of pleasure from watching the fireworks.'

Sarah could tell by the expressions on everyone's faces that they thought the same and because Olga was such a snob, and had been nasty to the youngsters, they'd targeted her on purpose.

A conversation struck up about Bonfire night and she listened to Mark expressing his concern that an old lady shouldn't feel threatened in her home and how the police should be out patrolling on the streets more. Once again, she thought, what a caring, considerate man he was.

The session got underway with a big discussion at the end about the texture of the turkey and each sample was marked from tough-to chewy-to tender, in a descending order. Sarah talked through the cooking instructions. Olga and Margaret were particularly interested because they were used to cooking large whole turkeys at a low heat and for a long time.

'Usually, I can tell when I'm carving the turkey how tender and moist it's going to be,' Mark said. 'Or whether it's been over cooked and is dry.'

Olga nodded. 'It is tricky to get it exactly right. We have an electric carving knife, and my husband was a grand carver,' she said pulling back her shoulders.

Rebecca tittered at this comment and received a glower of disapproval from Olga. Sarah decided, these two were never going to get along together no matter how many sessions they did.

Mark interrupted. 'I'm not sure if it's just a Northern tradition but the man in the family usually carves the turkey in our families,' he said looking around the table.

'Heavens,' Jason said and snorted. 'I've never heard of that. In Falkirk where I was brought up with five brothers, they'd be a fight every year.'

Everyone laughed, collected their vouchers, and slowly left the room.

Chapter Eight – Friday 9th November

Jason left the taste panel room thinking of his brothers and how happy Christmas mornings had always been at home. He still missed them all every day and at the age of twenty-three he struggled to come to terms with how much had happened since leaving home.

Over the last three weeks when he'd left the taste panel room, he had walked past a pub where men gathered outside which looked inviting. But now, he decided that the constant torture of, will I, won't I, was too much to bear and took a different route home.

He knew that the first time he weakened and went inside the pub would be the start of a different life and the fall-out from his actions would be catastrophic. But he also knew that sometimes the temptation was so overwhelming it would only be a matter of time before he lost control.

Putting his key in the front door of their small two-bedroomed flat, he heard Stacey call out, 'Is that you?'

Now, her strong Glaswegian accent shamefully grated upon him like never before. Within six months of marriage and two babies, who at the minute cried day and night, he knew he'd made the biggest mistake of his life.

'No,' he said in a mocking tone. 'It's Jack the Ripper.'

She turned to look at him from her seat in front of the TV where she was engrossed in EastEnders. 'Ha, bloody, ha,' she muttered. 'You'd be just as glad if you came back one night, and I had been hacked to death by the ripper then you wouldn't have a guilty conscience about ignoring me in bed.'

He sighed heavily. Her face, which he once thought cute, was now twisted into an ugly sneer.

'Don't start,' he warned. 'I'm totally done in.'

Looking around the stark bare walls of the rented flat he knew he should decorate or do home improvements for his family. But he felt weary at the thought of it. They'd chosen the flat because it was the biggest out of three available for their budget and had made optimistic plans about the changes they could make. But by the time the girls arrived they had been broke and were now living from one month to another counting every penny.

She stood up and pulled her shoulders back ready for another argument and his heart sank with dread. He hated any type of confrontation and especially with Stacey. In the past he'd agreed to anything just to keep the peace. But lately, agreeing to have sex with her had turned from a chore into an event which left him feeling physically sick.

Luckily one of the girls started to cry and she shouted, 'Now look what you've done! They've been asleep for over an hour.'

'I'll see to them,' he muttered. 'You watch the TV.'

They usually took turns to see to the girls and because he'd been awake for half of the night, he knew it should be her turn. However, the girls had turned into a get out of an argument clause and he padded along to their bedroom.

He picked up his eldest daughter and cuddled her to his chest. She immediately opened her eyes and gave him such a toothless gappy-grin that his heart melted. Her sister was still asleep, and he pulled the blanket up over her chubby legs then smiled.

They were the main reason he didn't dare set foot into that pub, or come out, as everyone said.

Sitting in the wicker chair next to the cot he spun the pink elephant mobile which made her gurgle. It was a sound he would treasure for the rest of his life. He stared at the half painted pink wall and closed his tired eyes then groaned. How and when had it got so out of hand that he was in this miserable existence which he called his life.

He'd known since the age of seventeen that he liked to look at men more than women and had fought then struggled against his feelings. But, at the age of twenty, and after one fantastic night with a travelling salesman, he knew for certain that it was right for him. It had been, and still was, the best night of his life.

Not another living soul knew, and he had never seen the guy again. All he'd known was that he wanted more. The feelings of entrapment living in Falkirk with his family of brothers was all-consuming. They had all married and when his parents lined him up with a friend's daughter, he knew he had to get away.

The thought of his brothers finding out was terrifying. He'd also known the shame would destroy his mother so when the bank offered him a transfer to North Shields he had gladly accepted. At the time, he'd thought it would be a chance to explore his sexuality in secret.

His daughter whimpered and he snapped his eyes open as if they were on an automatic pulley system. Her sleepy eyelids then closed again, and he carefully lifted her back into her cot tucking the pink blanket around her tiny body.

When he stood up, he saw Stacey in the doorway and slowly moved towards her. Her ginger-red hair was dishevelled, and she wore the same old dressing gown with stains down the front. The perpetual scowl on her face said it all.

The night they'd met he thought she was quite pretty and full of fun. She'd been working in the estate agents in North Shields for three years and had a wide circle of friends. Stacy had included him in her social life which had helped him settle because at first, he'd felt lonely living in a single bedsit. After a few dates he consoled himself with the fact that it was just a casual fling, and he was doing no harm. But then after one drunken night of what he could only call

half-hearted sex, she was pregnant with the twins. He'd
found himself caught up in the throes of wedding plans, and
when a bus load of Scots was booked to come down for the
wedding, he simply hadn't known how to stop it all.

'Fancy an early night?' she asked winking at him.

He turned to walk past her. 'Nah, I'm knackered,' he said.
'I was up half of the night and it's catching up on me now.'

She put her arm across the doorway to stop him and he
sighed heavily. 'Don't Stacey, not tonight!'

She snapped. 'Not tonight!' She yelled. 'It's never any
night, it's over two months since you've touched me.'

'I…I just can't help it,' he stuttered and moved her arm to
walk down the hall.

She followed him hissing, 'You're having an affair, aren't
you? I can smell perfume on your shirt. Who is she?'

He wanted to howl with laughter. Slowly and deliberately,
he said. 'No, I'm not seeing anyone. If you can smell
anything on my shirt it will be turkey because that's what
we've been tasting at the panel.'

'You're a liar!' she shouted following him to their
bedroom.

Taking a deep breath, he sat on the end of the bed and
counted slowly to five. He often felt that one day a monster
would burst out of his body and run amok because of the
constant restraint.

Striping his shirt and trousers off he pulled on pyjama
bottoms. 'Ssh, you'll wake the girls,' he said. 'I've told you
about everyone at the panel and I did come straight home
tonight.'

'Well, you didn't last week,' she hissed again. 'You went
to the pub with them!'

He sighed. 'Yeah, and I told you all about Ayesha, Sarah,
Rebecca and old Margaret. If I were having an affair with

one of the women, would I tell you all about them? And, I have asked you to join us one night.'

She slumped down on the opposite end of the bed. 'Well, why?' she asked. 'Why don't you fancy me anymore? Have I changed that much since the girls were born?'

The guilt surged through him, and he knew his rebuff was causing her grief. Her confidence was shattered which wasn't fair, but the alternative didn't bear thinking about.

'Look,' he said taking another deep breath. 'It's not you. It's got nothing to do with you. It's me. I'm just knackered looking after them all day.'

She laid a hand on his bare shoulder, and he tried hard not to flinch.

'Well,' she said. 'It was a joint decision for me to go back to work because I earn more than you. But if you want to switch around again, I'll stay home to bring them up.'

Thinking about this option, he decided it would mean even less freedom because while she was at work and the babies slept, he trawled the internet looking at men on websites. Not being able to do this scared him. Sometimes, it was the only thing that kept him going.

He said, 'No, let's just leave it a while and see how we go. This teething can't last forever.'

She pulled the duvet back and crawled underneath yawning. 'Okay,' she said. 'As soon as they wake during the night call me, and I'll take the next two turns so you can catch up on some sleep.'

He looked down at her riddled with guilt. It was mostly his fault that they were in this situation and his stomach churned. Although, she shouldered the responsibility for contraception and getting pregnant in the first place, once it had happened, he'd been in complete agreement that an abortion wasn't even on their radar.

***

Stacey walked into the estate agents the next morning and clashed the door. Her two colleagues looked up startled at the noise.

Amanda sat at one of three desks in the square modern office, and asked, 'What's up? Bad night?'

Stacey removed her coat and hung it up on the metal stand behind her desk. She sighed heavily. 'Oh, just the usual knock-back, again!'

Amanda got up from her desk and crossed the room. 'Did you have it out with him?'

'Well, yes. I asked him about the lack of bedroom action, and he swears he's not having an affair. He reckons it's not my fault but that he's just worn out looking after the girls,' Stacey said. 'But it's humiliating having to ask for it, I mean, why the hell doesn't he want to do it anymore?'

Amanda smiled. 'And you believe him?'

'He sounds convincing,' Stacey said shrugging her shoulders. 'And I suppose I have to really because I've got no proof either way.'

Amanda tutted. 'All I know is that if a man is not interested in you then it means he's getting it somewhere else. They're all hard-wired in that department, believe me. I can't go more than three days before my Alan is pulling at my nighty,' she said. 'Look, I'm making coffee, do you want one?'

Stacey nodded and headed into the toilets. Gripping the edge of the sink she stared into the mirror at the dark circles under her eyes. How had she ended up in this sham of a marriage? She moaned and knew deep down inside that Jason didn't love her.

When she'd first met him, she found him good fun and he'd fitted in well with her friends. One by one all of couples had started to settle down, get engaged, and save up for their weddings. And she'd wanted to be the same. The thought of reaching her late twenties and being alone without at least a steady boyfriend was scary. She remembered the day she realised she was pregnant and although she hadn't exactly planned it, she had been lax with her pill. Of course, she hadn't confessed that to Jason and thankfully, he had believed every word she'd told him.

Returning to her desk she sipped the coffee whilst making a plan of action. She knew Amanda was right. He had to be having an affair and if it wasn't one of the women from his supermarket sessions then he must be meeting someone elsewhere.

She gritted her teeth at the thought of him making love to another woman while she sat at home frustrated with the babies. Stacey thought of everything she'd done for him when he first arrived in North Shields and their happy wedding day with both their families. She chewed her fingernail knowing she had to find out who this other woman was.

There was no way they were going to make a fool out of her, she vowed. And the only way she could get any definite proof was to follow him on a Thursday night. If he entered the supermarket building, then at least she would know it was one of the women in the group. She'd find out who it was, by God, she would.

Chapter Nine - Thursday 15th November

'Well, it sounds to me as though he's definitely interested,' Christine said to Sarah as they sat in her lounge sharing a bottle of red Merlot. She'd skipped the gym and had gone straight home to shower off the smell of turkey before Christine arrived.

'Do you think so?' Sarah asked. 'I thought at first when he arrived early it was a genuine excuse. But when he probed me about a partner at Christmas, well, I had second thoughts.'

Christine grinned and sank back into the soft leather settee. 'Of course, he came early on purpose. But there again, who wouldn't be interested in either of us delectable babes!'

'I know,' Sarah giggled feeling a little tipsy. 'But seriously though, you were right a few weeks ago when you said it was far too soon.'

'Hmm,' Christine muttered. 'But you do have to start again sometime and if he's a nice guy then maybe he'll be good to practise on before your next hunk comes along.'

Sarah smiled at her friend's confidence in the fact that there would always be men around no matter what age they were.

'Oh, he is a nice man. In fact, too nice. I couldn't use him like that. Especially not with Rebecca breathing down my neck.'

Christine pursed her lips. 'Next week you have to find out exactly what is going on between them and whether Mark is telling the truth. She sounds like a desperately sad divorcee trying to get her claws into husband number two.'

'But what if she isn't? And what if she genuinely likes Mark? And, what if it is him that is stringing her along with dates and promises,' she said. 'You see, I don't have much trust left in men especially after what Paul did.'

Christine squeezed her shoulder. 'That's more than understandable. Just take it easy and see what happens at the next session.'

***

At the taste panel while Sarah placed the packs of trifles down the centre of the table Ayesha, Jason and Margaret arrived and sat in their usual places. Ayesha was talking openly now about the arranged marriage and told them how she'd sat up late sewing wedding outfits and helping her mother with the plans.

'It's such a shame,' Margaret said quietly and picked at the skin around her thumb nail. 'Your wedding day should be the happiest day of your life. Mine certainly was. It didn't last of course but I did enjoy the whole day.'

Jason put his arm around Ayesha to comfort her. 'There's still a while to go yet.'

Olga rubbed her gnarled fingers which looked swollen with arthritis. She asked, 'Is this happening because of your family's religious beliefs, and is your father actually allowed to do this to you?'

Sarah could see Ayesha raise her shoulders and knew she would feel the same. It was one thing for Ayesha to berate her family, but she had to defend them when someone else was criticising.

Ayesha explained, 'It is part of the Hindu culture and usually works quite well if you are both Indian and agree to the marriage. But I'm half English and some of it is my fault because I don't want to conform.'

Jason only looked about five foot five, but he seemed to raise himself up on the chair and glowered at Olga. 'It doesn't matter what faith you hold it's never right to be forced into a situation against your will that you aren't happy with,' he said. 'I know quite a bit about wanting to break away from traditions and being true to yourself.'

Sarah could tell that the rest of the group were wondering what he meant because she was too.

'If I may,' Rebecca interrupted. 'Jason told us earlier about the law changing soon which is something I'd have to look into because I'm not up to scratch on that. But I could find help groups or associations for you to contact. Then you might not feel as though you're fighting the battle all on your own?'

Relief flooded Ayesha's face. 'That would be great, but my father mustn't know. If he found out, well, let's just say, I wouldn't want to upset him even further,' she said and fidgeted with the thin gold bangles on her wrist. They made a twinkling noise, and she lowered her eyes.

Rebecca leant forward across the table and said, 'Ayesha, anything you and I talk about will always be strictly confidential.'

She nodded and put her hands together in a thank you sign.

Mark said, 'And you're never on your own here, Ayesha. You are amongst friends who are willing to help. Well, I know I certainly am.'

There was a consensus of agreement from everyone, even Olga, although it was said with a hunch of her shoulders. Sarah decided it was time to move the group session forward and away from the heated subject.

'Now, this week's session will be a little more complicated. I'd like you to fill in one form for each component in each trifle,' Sarah said. 'If you remember on the first week, we had filling and pastry in the tarts which was two components but then the sausages and turkey were just meat so that was only one component.'

Margaret and Jason looked puzzled, so she continued, 'But in a trifle we have fruit, jelly, sponge, sherry, custard, cream and toasted almonds, which is seven components or layers, to make up the whole trifle.'

Everyone nodded then in understanding and Sarah smiled. 'So, we'll eat the sample of trifle as it is spooned out of the bowl but then as an extra assessment we will split the sponge, cream, and custard, etc, to comment upon them all separately. This will tell us, for example, if the sponge is too dry and spoils the whole product or if the cream is too sloppy to hold its decoration and pattern on the top.'

Margaret clapped her hands. 'What a clever idea, Sarah. It's amazing what you managers do to make sure we get the best,' she said then flushed at her outburst.

This was what Sarah had hoped to see in Margaret. Her interest in the panel had overridden her nerves when speaking in front of the group.

Olga said, 'There's nothing worse than dry sponge, it spoils the whole trifle. And it's such an easy task to soak it in sherry, I've been doing it for years.'

'Thank you, Margaret,' Sarah said. 'And, you are right, Olga, but we must remember that these trifles are not made in a kitchen, one or two at a time. Especially at Christmas our suppliers make thousands all day and night in factories. Therefore, soaking sponge the day before might be quite a challenge for them.'

She could tell Mark was interested by the way he raised his eyebrows.

'Really?' He asked, 'And how do they keep up with production and have it ready for the week before Christmas?'

Sarah smiled at him allowing herself a gaze into his brown eyes. 'Well now, that is the fifty-thousand-dollar question that has production managers up and down this country nearly tearing their hair out!'

Everyone laughed and she continued. 'Seriously though, we put our orders in two months in advance so the suppliers know exactly how much they have to make for us but if a product is a great seller we could run out and have to ask them to make more. Or we can be left with unsold stock if everyone decides they are sick of sherry trifle this Christmas and fancy a change.'

Rebecca said. 'Hmm, I couldn't imagine Christmas without sherry trifle, turkey, and all the usual traditional things we eat. I suppose the marketing managers and buyers have to depend upon the fact that we English will always be set in our ways.'

Sarah grinned with pleasure to see everyone interested in the reasoning behind the taste panels and weren't just coming along to eat for free and get their vouchers. It made her job and the extra nightly sessions truly worthwhile.

After they'd all tasted the trifles, Sarah held up each pack of trifle and asked everyone to check the layers. 'We need to make sure each layer is separate and the one thing we don't want to see for example, is the custard running into the cream or that the sponge has sunken to the bottom or that there is no fruit visible.'

Comments were agreed upon and written on the forms and then Sarah scooped and separated the components one by one while everyone marked their scores. The toasted almonds were the last to assess and she gave them all one each on a plate double checking first that nobody had nut allergies.

Rebecca selected a large almond flake and tapped Mark's arm; he turned his head towards her. Unexpectedly, she tried to seductively pop the almond into his mouth. Sarah watched in amusement because his face looked horrified at the gesture.

'W…what the!!' He spluttered and spat the almond out into his napkin. 'What the hell are you doing?' he asked and looked very cross.

Jason whooped with laughter saying, 'Hey, Mark, are you trying to be a proper taster by spitting it out?'

Everyone joined in the laughter while Mark's cheeks flushed. He glared at Rebecca who tried pathetically to flutter her eyelashes.

Sarah decided Christine was right. Rebecca was simply a sad and desperate divorcee. She felt sorry for her and hoped in years to come that she didn't end up like Rebecca, desperate for a man's attention.

For the rest of the session Mark sat with his back to Rebecca and completely ignored her mutterings of apologies, which gave Sarah renewed hope.

She'd brought extra samples of the trifles knowing she would be separating the layers and because there were three whole trifles that hadn't been opened, she asked, 'These will probably be thrown out, does anyone want to take one home?'

Rebecca shook her head. 'I've got my figure to watch and couldn't possibly eat a whole trifle to myself unless anyone wants to share it with me?'

She looked at Mark who got up abruptly from the table, made his excuses and took his voucher.

Jason smiled and took a trifle.

Margaret said, 'Well, if no one else wants the last two I'll take them for tomorrow for the Women's Institute ladies when we have our coffee break.'

Chapter Ten – Friday 16th November

Only five more taste panels left before Christmas, Margaret thought and shivered in the cold north wind. She opened the front door to her small, two-up, two-down terraced house on Roseberry Avenue. Remembering last year's expensive gas bill, she resisted the urge to switch on the central heating but hurried through into the lounge and turned the gas fire up high then made a pot of tea. Settling herself in her favourite armchair in front of the old fireplace she sipped the hot tea.

She'd loved the trifle tasting they'd done this evening but above all, she loved the fact that she was included in their company. Even to the extent that she was beginning to feel less self-conscious when speaking, which was a miracle. She was delighted to think of them as her new friends now. Well, maybe not, Rebecca, although she had been kinder to her today, but she knew deep down that the lawyer thought her a silly old woman.

The young women now-a-days were different to how she'd been in her thirties. She glanced apprehensively at the unopened letter on the mantelpiece. The women were full of confidence, independent and outgoing whereas she'd always been shy, quiet, and lacking in any type of self-belief.

Both her parents had been killed during the Second World War when a single bomb from a lone enemy aircraft scored a hit on Wilkinson's lemonade factory. The basement had been used as a public air raid shelter and there'd been 107 people killed. Miraculously she'd survived and had been raised by her aunt and uncle until she had met and married Jack.

Jack-the-lad everyone had called him, and her aunt had been horrified when she'd started to court him. But her aunt hadn't known how her uncle used to press himself up against her when he came home drunk from the pub. And Margaret, at the age of sixteen, had decided that Jack was the lesser of the two evils.

She glanced up again at the letter which was post-marked from The Isle of Man knowing it was from her youngest son, Peter. It had arrived yesterday, but she hadn't felt strong enough to open it and read the curt refusal that she knew it would contain.

She wrote the same every year almost begging Peter and his family to come for a Christmas visit but it was four years now since he'd accepted. It broke her heart to think of her two grandsons. One of which she'd never met because he had been born after the last visit, and the oldest being eleven in January. Taking the envelope from the fireplace she drained her tea and wondered what the excuse would be this year while tearing the envelope and reading the letter.

The excuse, however, was a double blow because he was taking his family over to his brother, Geoffrey's house in Australia for Christmas. Oh dear, she moaned quietly and felt tears slide down her cheeks.

She'd never once been invited to Australia since he emigrated and had only received one or two letters in the first couple of years. Then not another word since. Her whole family would be together celebrating without her, and she felt mortified at the slight. So much so that it caused a tightness across her chest which made her catch her breath.

Putting her head back against the chair she went over, the argument, again in her mind. She called it, the argument, because she knew since then the relationship with her sons had never been the same.

'It's all your fault, you stupid woman!' Peter had shouted at her in his teenage-husky voice.

She'd been shocked at the word stupid more than anything else. 'What? So, it's my fault that your father left?' Margaret had pleaded. 'How on earth do you work that out?'

He'd come up close to her face and she had looked into the same grey eyes she saw every time she looked in the mirror.

'Because I saw you! I came downstairs and I hid behind the door. I saw you sitting there crying and whinging at Dad. He'd shouted that he couldn't stand anymore of your carry-on and stormed out then left us!'

Margaret's stomach had churned. He'd only been six years old. How much had he seen? 'A…and how long were you behind the door before he left,' she'd stuttered just as Geoffrey came into the room to stand behind him.

Peter had pulled his broad shoulders back defiantly. 'Just what I told you. But I didn't need to see anymore. He left because he couldn't stand you! And we've never had our dad with us because of that!'

She had breathed a sigh of relief. Thankfully, he hadn't seen his dad swipe her across the face so hard that she'd thought her jaw was broken. No matter what they thought of her she hadn't wanted to ruin the memories of their dad. But she hadn't retaliated.

At the age of eighteen Geoffrey had sneered and she'd gasped in shock at how much like Jack he'd looked. He had been his father's son through and through. He raged, 'So, why were you having a go at him and whinging?'

'Because he'd gambled all his wages on a horse and we had nothing left,' she'd stated. 'I hadn't a penny to buy food for us, that's why.'

Geoffrey had just finished his apprenticeship and was a qualified plumber. He'd laughed. 'But that is what we do, us men. We work hard and drink hard then spend our money on what we see fit. And, if that means a little flutter on the horses, well so be it.'

She hadn't reacted any further and nothing more was ever said about, the argument, but from that day neither of her sons had ever been the same around her. The good morning or good night wishes had stopped, and a polite silence had settled in the house.

She'd tried a couple of times to talk to Peter afterwards but had received shrugs of his shoulders and given up. A year later Geoffrey had gone off to Australia with a building contractor and never returned. Peter then met a girl in Newcastle when he was nineteen and had moved to The Isle of Man.

***

The next morning, she walked through Preston Village, past Post Office Lane towards the village hall for the WI meeting. She heard her friend, Dorothy calling her name and turned to see her cross the road.

'Goodness, you were walking at some pace?' Dorothy said catching up with her.

Margaret smiled. 'Was I?' she asked. 'I didn't realise. The cold is nipping at my fingers on this handle, so I thought I'd hurry.'

Dorothy smiled and linked her arm through Margaret's while they walked and scolded her for not wearing gloves. Margaret told her about the trifle she had and entering the large old hall with the inadequate heating system they decided to keep their coats on until others arrived.

It was a large room with a small stage at the front and green plastic chairs set out with an aisle down the centre. They always sat on the left side with their other friends. Dorothy was Margaret's oldest friend and she thought of her as the sister she never had.

'What's happened?' Dorothy asked. 'And don't give me any of that flannel that there's nothing wrong!'

Margaret smiled weakly. 'I had a letter from Peter saying he's not coming for Christmas again.'

Dorothy exclaimed, 'I knew it! Those blooming lads, I would like to get my hands on them. They'd get the length of my tongue, all right!'

Margaret knew she was just the woman to do this and smiled with fondness at Dorothy's tiny five-foot frame in a camel coat and brown bobble-wool hat. Her bright blue eyes sparkled from a heavily wrinkled face with two long hairs growing out of a mole on her chin. Even at the age of seventy she still ruled her family with an iron rod. Dorothy's son of six foot four told Margaret last year he was still terrified of her which had made her giggle.

'And, to make matters worse he's going over to Australia to see Geoffrey, so they'll all be together.'

Dorothy mellowed. 'Aah, Margie,' she muttered using her old nickname. 'They are wasters, the pair of them. They should be flogged for upsetting you like this.'

Margaret bristled slightly. 'Well, they don't know I'm upset about not seeing them. I never tell them that. So, maybe they think I'm okay and don't mind not being invited. I mean, Geoffrey might think I'm too old to fly all the way across to Australia?'

Dorothy shook her head slowly. 'When are you ever going to stop defending the little blighters?'

Margaret could feel tears sting the back of her eyes. 'Probably when they lower me down into my grave,' she said and choked back tears. Dorothy squeezed her hand in support.

The room began to fill up with more of their friends and Olga arrived nodding hello but sat on the opposite side of the hall with the committee members. The meeting began with two speakers who came and went in a blur to Margaret while she looked at Dorothy thinking about their friendship.

They'd started school together, met their husbands at the same dance and the following year had planned their weddings. The only difference was that Dorothy had chosen a good man not like her Jack.

It was Dorothy who'd held her hand in hospital when Jack had beaten her. The boys had been too little to leave in the house and Dorothy had shielded them in her own home. When Jack left, Dorothy helped her survive the years of scandal protecting her from the gossipmongers with her sharp wit and tongue. Margaret would always be eternally grateful.

They'd both worked at the local abattoir but because the wage wasn't enough to keep them Margaret had also cleaned in an evening for extra money.

The rousing female voices singing Jerusalem broke her thoughts and she joined in the chorus to which neither of them needed a song sheet. They'd been singing the song for so many years they were word perfect.

'You see, I'd felt sure Peter would come this year because I'd had that nice letter from his wife, Jane in the summer telling me all about their holiday,' Margaret said. 'And she'd ended the letter saying, hope to see you at Christmas.'

They followed all the other women into the coffee room adjacent to the hall.

Dorothy tutted shaking her head. 'Aye, he was lucky finding her, she's a nice lass. More than he deserves if you ask me. I still say you should have told them what a horrible bully Jack was,' she said and sat down on the end of a wood bench at the table.

Margaret sipped her coffee thoughtfully. 'I couldn't, well, not then. I didn't want to spoil their memories of him.

When they were little, we did have some good family times together.'

Dorothy raised an eyebrow while they scooped trifle into small dishes.

Feeling warmer Margaret slipped off her anorak. 'And, another thing,' she said quietly. 'I've had the spare room decorated with aeroplanes on the wallpaper because Jane said the little one loved flying and wants to be a pilot when he grows up.'

Dorothy smiled. 'Ah, well, that'll be easy painted over in a couple of years,' she said. 'And, you never know they might make it across next year.'

Olga appeared at the end of the small table and the ladies shuffled along the wood bench to make room for her. She squeezed herself down and sipped her coffee. Someone offered her trifle, but she declined giving them an account of the taste panel and how marvellous it had been to see the technologist specialising in her work.

Margaret had been pushed further along against Dorothy and she could feel her friend's shoulders stiffen with distaste while Olga spoke.

Dorothy had always hated Olga with a passion. And years ago, when Dorothy's husband had a small win on the pools, she'd offered Margaret money to give up her cleaning job at Olga's house.

Olga said to Margaret. 'So, have you spent your vouchers yet? That pantry of yours must be bursting with extra provisions that'll go to waste for yet another year.'

Margaret floundered, 'W…well, I haven't spent them all yet.'

Dorothy pulled her shoulders back ready for battle and interrupted. 'Oh, it won't be wasted, Olga,' she said. 'Margaret has so many friends that will call over Christmas that it'll all be eaten. You don't need to worry on that score.'

Olga tutted and took a deep breath to fire another comment back but Margaret, hating confrontation, changed the subject and discussed the latest win at the bingo hall and what had happened in Coronation Street.

***

When they'd finished their coffee, Margaret and Dorothy left the hall to walk back through the village together.

Dorothy seethed. 'That blooming woman! I can't stand her. Who on earth does Olga think she is? She pretends to be so high and mighty which is a hoot, especially for someone who at sixteen years old couldn't keep her legs shut!'

'Sssh,' Margaret whispered. 'Somebody might hear you!'

Chapter Eleven – Thursday 22nd November

'It wasn't exactly a lunch date,' Mark said to Sarah while she emptied small tubs of prawn cocktails into numbered dishes. They were in the small kitchen of the taste panel room where he'd arrived early again. He had followed her into the kitchen with an excuse to help carry the cocktails.

Her heart began to race because he was standing so close to her, and she inhaled his slightly spicy aftershave. 'Oh?' She asked, 'So, it wasn't arranged?'

He smiled. 'I just wanted to put this out there because Margaret seems to have given everyone the impression, including you, that we are dating. But we are most certainly not. She just turned up in my shop the day after week one and asked me to join her for a quick bite on her lunch break.'

Sarah worked around him peeling plastic from the tops of the tubs and using a different spoon for each sample. 'And you haven't been seeing each other apart from the lunch date?'

'Well, we had a quick drink in the pub the following week. But within an hour of her company, I realised she's not my kind of woman,' he said. 'Then last week after the almond fiasco, well, let's just say I'll be giving her a wide berth from now. Although I do feel sorry for her and have tried to help with support for her mam because she's dying. But to be perfectly honest, Rebecca intimidates me more than anything else.'

'Intimidates you?' Sarah asked and giggled. 'You don't seem the type of guy who would be easily threatened.'

He raised an eyebrow. 'Aah, now I can tell you've formed entirely the wrong opinion of me. I'm completely lost when it comes to women and dating,' he said. 'I was with Jessie all my life and now I want to start again, I haven't a clue.'

Sarah looked into his eyes and felt giddy with her heart racing. He stared back at her and slowly moved his hand along the bench towards her when suddenly the hatch door was opened from the room side and Margaret stuck her head through. They instantly jumped apart.

Margaret grinned at them with a smug expression on her face. 'Em, sorry to interrupt but can I make some tea?'

'Yes, Margaret, of course you can,' Sarah said and bit her lip. 'I was just getting the prawn cocktails ready, and Mark is going to help carry them through.'

Mark gave a small grunt clearing his throat then picked up two dishes and went into the room.

Margaret practically skipped her way into the kitchen to switch on the kettle. While Sarah had been so engrossed with Mark, she hadn't realised everyone had arrived and chastised herself for losing her professional lead on the group. She must keep her feelings for Mark separate when she was working, she thought and busied herself with forms while Mark brought all five samples to the table.

Rebecca had sat in her usual seat but after Mark placed the last dish down onto the table he walked around to the opposite end and sat down next to Ayesha. Which was where Margaret usually sat.

There were audible gasps from everyone. So, when Margaret arrived at the room, she almost dropped the tea tray with surprise. However, she swiftly recovered herself, placed the tray onto the table and took the spare seat next to Rebecca.

Sarah thought Rebecca would be furious, but she didn't seem too perturbed. She seemed to have a glazed look in her eyes as though she was miles away in another place altogether.

Olga leaned forward towards the samples and exclaimed, 'Hmm, what a lovely fresh smell.'

Sarah explained what size prawns were used in each pot and how they would note the difference in the flavours of the cocktail sauce because each supermarket had their own recipe.

'My mam loves prawns,' Rebecca muttered quietly. 'Not that she'll be able to enjoy them anymore.'

Everyone looked at her while two big fat tears slowly rolled down her cheek and she uttered a small choking noise. Sarah could tell she was desperately trying to keep her tears at bay.

Margaret instantly put her arm along Rebecca's shoulders. 'Oh, my dear. What's wrong?'

Rebecca began to sob, and Margaret fished around in her bag for tissues. But Ayesha beat her to it and hurried to them with a pocket-size pack of tissues.

Mark and Jason looked at each other and she saw Jason shrug his slight shoulders. Sarah laid the spoon down that she had ready to serve the first sample.

'S…she's unconscious now,' Rebecca stuttered in between sobs. 'And the staff in the hospice have told me it will only be a matter of days. I've sat with her for nine hours but then left to go home and rest. But when I got back to the house it was so empty and quiet, I couldn't stand it.'

Sarah was shocked at the outburst from Rebecca's usual cool and collected demeanour. She said, 'But, Rebecca, you didn't need to come. It would be perfectly understandable that you would want to cancel the last few sessions and could have rung to say that.'

Rebecca wearily put her head onto Margaret's shoulder now and cried. 'I know but I didn't want to be home alone.'

Even Olga looked upset and asked, 'Have you no one who could stay with you?'

Rebecca sniffed and blew her nose trying to gain a sense of composure. 'Yes, my aunt is travelling up from Dorset tomorrow and another friend is arriving late tonight, but I just couldn't sit there thinking about her.'

Margaret soothed her and said, 'Of course, you couldn't. You did the right thing by coming here and as soon as we finish up, you'll come straight to my house until your friend arrives.'

Rebecca stared wide-eyed at Margaret.

Sarah could tell she was thinking the same. How could this old lady, who Rebecca on more than one occasion had been unpleasant to, be so kind.

Rebecca dried her face and lifted her head. 'Thank you, Margaret that is so kind of you,' she muttered. 'But I don't deserve such consideration from you.'

'Nonsense!' Margaret cried. 'I'd love to have you. And I'll tell you something else, your mam has been the luckiest woman in the world to have a daughter like you. I'd like to think there was someone who would weep over me like this when I'm on my way out.'

Olga clicked her tongue in obvious disapproval. 'What a load of rubbish you talk sometimes, Margaret,' she said. 'Rebecca doesn't need to listen to your hysterical ramblings.'

Sarah felt agitated because she could see the look of disgust on Mark, Jason, and Ayesha's faces while they glared at Olga.

Sarah sighed; she wasn't sure how to resolve the situation.

Rebecca cleared her throat and apologised. 'Sarah, I'm so sorry to disrupt everything. I'm fine now. Please continue with your panel.'

'Well,' Sarah said. 'Does everyone still want to take part?'

Olga retorted, 'Of course, we do. My mouth is watering at the smell of those prawns!'

Ayesha asked quietly, 'Is that okay with you, Rebecca? I wouldn't want you to think we are making light of your dreadful situation.'

Mark nodded, got up and walked back around to Rebecca. Sarah knew he must be feeling awful for moving his seat. He stood behind her and squeezed her shoulder sympathetically.

Rebecca nodded and patted Mark's hand. 'Of course, it is, and please forgive my outburst, let's just continue as normal,' she said.

Sarah spooned out prawn cocktails onto plates and the session got underway. Rebecca didn't taste the prawns but wrote down her comments about appearance and aroma to which Sarah smiled her thanks.

At the end Olga commented that the size of prawns was different in two of the pots.

'Yes, you've got it in one, Olga,' she said. 'We have to be careful when we are buying these products because we are naturally paying for the size and quality of the prawn. We write down exactly what we expect to get for our price in what's called a specification. Naturally, you will see more expensive prawn cocktails on the shelves with large tiger prawns and the price for these will sometimes be double what we pay for these smaller cold-water prawns.'

Mark asked. 'And what is the difference in these cold-water prawns to tiger prawns, other than the size, of course?'

Sarah explained, 'Well, cold-water prawns are small and caught in the Northeast Atlantic Sea which have a characteristic salty taste. Prawns are probably the only food group we have left that are sold by the pound and not the kilo. So, typically in this pot we will get 250 / 350 prawns to the pound whereas, in the two pots Olga mentioned which are tiny sandwich prawns there will be 500 / 600 to the pound. Tiger prawns, or another name which we use is warm-water prawns, are usually from Thailand or Indonesia where the sea is warmer. They are much bigger and meatier but do not have the salt flavour profile. These are bought in 75 / 80 to the pound.'

Everyone nodded and handed the forms back to her.

Olga puffed her chest out and said, 'Just what my late husband always used to say. You get what you pay for in life!'

There was an actual groan of annoyance from Jason and Olga looked at him sharply.

Jason's face was red, and Sarah saw him clench one of his small fists. 'Olga,' he said. 'Have you any control over the rubbish that comes out of your mouth?'

Margaret interrupted. 'Oh, Jason, Olga doesn't mean anything. It just comes out the wrong way sometimes.'

But Olga raised her large matronly frame up from the chair and wrinkled her large bulbous nose in the air as if the prawns had suddenly given off a bad odour. She grunted. 'Margaret, it's not necessary to make excuses for me. I'm perfectly entitled to my opinion and am never afraid to voice it. I do have my own high standards of living which I'm afraid there are very few young people can match now-a-days,' she said. And in an imperious manner she slung her long wool wrap around her shoulders and strode out of the room in full flow.

'Phew!' Sarah exclaimed laying the vouchers onto the table.

Relieved from Olga's exit everyone began to laugh and even Jason saw the funny side when Ayesha pulled a comical face imitating Olga's high and mighty expression.

Sarah heard Rebecca once again thanking Margaret for her kindness but told her she'd decided to go back to the hospice for another hour until her friend arrived.

Before she left the room Sarah saw Margaret push a voucher into the top of Rebecca's open handbag.

'Poor mite,' Margaret muttered to herself when the door closed behind Rebecca. 'She doesn't know what day of the week it is.'

Mark picked up his voucher winking mischievously at Sarah while holding out Margaret's anorak for her and offered her a lift home to which she tittered with pleasure.

Jason pulled his satchel over his shoulder and went off to buy more nappies with his voucher and Ayesha slid quietly out of the door behind him.

Sarah picked up the forms from the table and noticed on the top of Mark's form there was a post-it note stuck to the front which read, 'Please have dinner with me one night?'

Chapter Twelve – Friday 23rd November

When Olga reached home from the taste panel that night, she walked straight into the bathroom reached into the medicine cupboard and found the bottle of her strongest painkillers. The arthritic pain in her joints today had been unbearable and she knew that she had been even more unkind and priggish than usual. It was the constant pain all day and night which made her feel so crabby. And when something like listening to young Jason's Scottish accent irritated her, well, he was right, she did lose all control.

Dissolving the effervescent painkillers in a glass of water in the kitchen she automatically ran a finger along the window ledge looking for dust but like the rest of the house it was spotless. The cleaner she'd found last year when Margaret left was reasonable, but she was young and didn't have the same level of commitment to the job. She hardly spoke in conversation but simply moved from room-to-room dusting, vacuuming, and polishing with earphones plugged into a music device.

At least when Margaret used to clean, she'd work for a few hours then they'd have coffee and a chat. She had been someone to talk to twice a week. But now, unless she invited one of her few friends to visit, she was always on her own.

Taking the glass, she painfully put one foot in front of another and walked slowly into the lounge. The plodding noise of the square flat shoes she wore resounded on the wood floor. She swallowed the medicine then sat forward and eased her swollen tender feet from the shoes. Her toe joints were so badly twisted now they were the only shoes she could wear comfortably, and she hated them.

A photograph of herself and her husband, Philip, taken at a dinner dance when they were in their late twenties sat proudly on the cabinet. Olga smiled remembering the black patent stiletto heels she'd worn that night. The heels had clicked across the dance floor when they'd entered the ballroom and she had tingled with pleasure when everyone had turned to look.

The photograph was in black and white therefore, the colours of her emerald, green evening gown and white fur stole were faint but if she closed her eyes, she could remember every detail.

Philip had been a handsome man, and on occasions, she had been likened to Princess Margaret with her dark black hair and vivid blue eyes. She'd married well, or so her affluent parents repeatedly told her, and they'd been right because Philip had been a kind, gentle, diligent man for all their married life together.

She had never wanted for anything. If it had been within his power to give her what she'd wanted, he had. And she should have been able to love him. She should have made herself love him. But as hard as she'd tried, he could never take the place of her first love, Frank.

Frank had been what her mother classed unsuitable, but she had fallen for him the moment she'd looked into his deep brown eyes. They'd met in secret three times during which he'd made love to her with such passion it had stunned her young sixteen-year-old mind. Nothing since could match the intense feelings she'd experienced with Frank. After her father had chased him away, she had thought she would die from a broken heart.

'But I love him,' she'd cried sobbing. 'A…and he loves me!'

Her father had snarled. 'You stupid little idiot, you don't know the meaning of the word. If he did love you, he wouldn't have snatched the twenty pounds out of my hand that I've just offered him to clear off.'

Wrapping her arms around her body now, Olga moaned. She rocked herself backwards and forwards with the pain in her feet and felt tears prick her eyes with longing for those happy carefree days.

She turned on the TV set hoping the noise would combat the penetrating silence in the room and looked across at Philip's empty chair. The brown, velour upright chair stood in the corner of the large bay windowed room. Although it was two years since his sudden death on the golf course, she could still imagine him sitting cross legged with his glasses on the end of his nose and the newspaper spread upon his knee.

She didn't exactly miss Philip as her husband, but she did miss his friendship. Olga could tell that everyone at the taste panel felt sorry for Margaret who was visibly lonely and desperate for company. But if the truth were to be told, she felt lonelier than Margaret could ever be.

By noon, the following day she was rested and refreshed. The dining room was set ready for her lunch party. A white linen tablecloth had been ironed without a single crease. Matching place mats and napkins had been set for six people in the exact positions with small name cards. The silver cutlery and glasses sparkled and the central floral display of short-stemmed, white roses in a cut glass vase were beautifully arranged. She stood back glowing with pride then hurried upstairs to change before her guests arrived.

Olga loved superior quality clothes and slipped a new silk blouse over her head. The fitted silk hung beautifully over a pleated cream skirt. She'd been waiting for the right opportunity to wear them and today was the day, she thought then smiled. Turning from side to side in front of her full-length mirror she hoped the skirt flattered her ample bottom rather than accentuated it. When she was satisfied with the result, she kicked the flat shoes into the corner of the room and slipped her feet into cream, one-inch sling-backs. She knew she'd be in agony later but consoled herself with the fact that she could rest up with her painkillers.

Three fellow members of the resident's association arrived first and were sipping gin and tonics in the lounge when their local GP telephoned to say he'd be late.

'He must have been called out to an emergency,' Olga stated proudly to her guests. 'I think George will be glad when he can finally retire and hang up his stethoscope to call it a day.'

She tittered politely while the others laughed at her pun then hurried along the grand hallway to open the front door and greet her last guest, Reg, the chairman of the golf club.

'How lovely, Reg,' she gushed when he kissed her cheek and presented her with a bunch of flowers. 'Come through to the lounge we're having drinks.'

Reg had been an old friend of Philip's and was an encouraging flirt. Even for someone in his late sixties, he was manly with broad shoulders, thinning grey hair, and was always impeccably dressed.

When Philip was alive, Olga had thought that Reg had a twinkle in his eye for her but later dismissed this idea as fanciful nonsense because the men had been such great friends.

Reg had been devastated when Philip suddenly died. Since then, he'd asked if she would join him at the golf club for drinks, but she'd refused knowing it might be thought of as bad taste after her husband's death. However, as she followed him into the lounge now, she wondered if two years could be classed as a respectful length of time.

While they all sat around the long dining table with a late winter sun streaming through the big bay window onto the

Italian, gold-striped wallpaper she breathed a sigh of contentment. She knew the display of food was impressive and had used her vouchers towards the spread of salads, cooked meats, prawn cocktail, different varieties of bread and hand-curled pats of unsalted butter.

'You simply must try these quiche tarts,' she said to everyone handing the plate around the table. 'They were the first product we tried at the taste panels I've been going to on a Thursday evening.'

Reg grinned at her and helped himself to a large slice. 'It looks delicious,' he said. 'And are you enjoying the panels?'

Olga laid her knife and fork down and told them all about the sessions. How she enjoyed learning the research behind the products and, how professional and competent Sarah was.

'Her knowledge is commendable, she is efficient and dependable, and leads the group with such professionalism that it is a pleasure to be included. The other panellists however,' she said wrinkling her nose. 'Well, let's just say they leave a lot to be desired!'

Her guests nodded in understanding and Reg bellowed with laughter. 'Olga, you are such a card,' he said winking mischievously at her.

She explained how they collected the results and completed the forms commenting about the appearance, texture, smell, and aroma.

'And what size are these prawns?' Reg asked heaping a large spoonful of prawn cocktail onto his plate. 'I am partial to a big, fat juicy prawn.'

'That's outrageous, Reg,' she exclaimed giggling.

He grinned and popped the forkful of prawn cocktail into his mouth.

When everyone had finished lunch, she excused herself to go into the kitchen and collect the raspberry pavlova from the fridge. She hadn't heard anyone follow her down the hall but suddenly she felt a presence behind her and spun around to see Reg.

He smiled. 'Can I help?' He asked holding out his hands for the large bowl.

'Yes, please,' she said flustered with his closeness and handed him the bowl.

He laid it onto the bench then leaned close to her ear. 'You look simply ravishing today, darling,' he whispered. 'When are you going to come up to the club and have dinner with me?'

Feeling her cheeks flush her stomach did a quick somersault. She felt like a young woman again and playfully patted his arm. 'Well, now, Reg, that might just be sooner than you think,' she teased.

'Splendid, absolutely splendid,' he retorted.

He picked up the bowl in one hand then as he walked past her, he used his other hand to pat her bottom to which she gave a small squeal of delight.

When lunch ended and she stood at the front door with Reg waving goodbye to her other guests, he brushed her cheek with a small kiss. 'So, Thursday at 7.30?'

'Looking forward to it,' she whispered.

She gave him her best smile when he hopped from the bottom step onto the drive and jauntily set off down the road whistling.

Closing the front door, she leaned back against it hugging herself with anticipation. Sorry Philip, she muttered and looked up to the ceiling then went into the dining room to clear the dishes.

The following morning when she picked the post out of the wire basket on the back of the red front door she puzzled at a plain brown envelope. Opening the envelope, she wandered into the kitchen and skim-read the letter standing in front of the window overlooking the large garden.

The words seemed to dance around on the page as they registered in her brain, and she grabbed the edge of the bench to stop herself from falling. But nobody knew, she floundered, how could they? It had been over forty years ago? Even Philip hadn't known.

Digesting the news her whole body began to tremble and her stomach churned. She felt physically sick with the revelation. Groping behind herself for a wood chair she slumped down and with shaking hands re-read the letter slowly and carefully.

Chapter Thirteen – Thursday 29th November

While Mark, Olga, Ayesha, Jason, and Margaret sat around the table, Sarah rushed into the room breathless from running up the stairs. 'Sorry, everyone,' she apologised. 'I was just leaving the office when Rebecca rang to say her mam died last night and she won't be coming this week. I didn't want to appear rude and cut her short because I was running late.'

Margaret gushed, 'Oh, dear. Of course, you couldn't. Come and sit down, catch your breath and I'll pour you some tea.'

Mark got up and took the bag of samples from Sarah's hand. 'Here, give them to me and I'll put them in the kitchen for you.'

She beamed her thanks at him and sipped the tea. 'Apparently she died peacefully at nine o'clock last night and Rebecca and her aunt were sitting with her,' she said. 'Rebecca sounded tearful, of course, but not agitated and panicky like she was last week.'

'Well, it would probably be a relief because she's lain unconscious for so long,' Jason said as Mark walked back into the room.

Taking his seat, Mark nodded. 'I suppose it can be thought of as relief. But the Macmillan nurse told me with Jessie that even though you are expecting it to happen and think you're prepared, when it does happen it's still a shock, which it was.'

Margaret took a tissue from inside her sleeve. 'Poor little mite,' she said and blew her nose. 'She won't know what's hit her and now she'll have the funeral to arrange and the house to sort out.'

Mark said, 'Well, I think Rebecca has done a lot of the paperwork already. She told me her mam had asked her to go through insurance policies, house deeds, and loads of old documents she had in the attic.'

Sarah could tell he'd stopped himself from saying anymore on the subject and she wondered what else he knew.

Olga said, 'Her mam would probably have wanted everything to be in place for when her time came. I know I would. And it's best, no matter how upsetting it is, to have things organised.'

Sarah excused herself and headed into the kitchen to open the tubs of custard while she heard Margaret suggesting they could send a sympathy card and flowers to Rebecca.

Heating the samples of custard in the microwaves she looked through the hatch at the group of people she'd become familiar with over the last seven weeks. She marvelled at how willingly they'd give money for Rebecca at her time of grief.

Jason was in the process of growing a long handlebar moustache and had a small black cap perched on the back of his head. The jeans he wore seemed even slimmer and tighter than ever with a huge hipster buckle. Sarah decided his look of dog-tired had been replaced with a definite twinkle in his eye.

Ayesha looked more upbeat than previous weeks and she'd overheard her telling Margaret that her friend, Becky was going to accompany her to one of the support groups that Rebecca had recommended. Her outfit this week was in chocolate brown and gold. Sarah wondered if there was any colour scheme that didn't suit Ayesha, but she supposed when you had such striking good looks, you'd look good in anything.

Margaret and Olga had their heads together and were talking quietly in hushed tones. Sarah thought Olga seemed a little down this week as though she had pressing worries.

She certainly didn't appear her usual feisty self. And whatever it was they were discussing Margaret wore a look of friendly concern while she listened to Olga.

And Mark, well he looked simply great, she thought dreamily. She needed to find a time in the session to agree to his dinner date. It would have to be when the others weren't listening because she didn't want them to know. And she did not want to embarrass him either because he was a private type of guy and had hated Rebecca's flirting in previous weeks.

Maybe at the end she could think of an excuse for him to stay behind but then this too might arouse suspicion. Carrying the first sample bowls of custard through to the room she had an idea.

Taking a pen from her brief case she scribbled on the inside of one of the panel forms, 'I'd love to. How about the new Indian restaurant?'

She walked around the table laying a form in front of everyone.

'So, we have custard this week,' she said and winked at Mark.

He picked his form up, put his glasses on and turned the form over. She could tell from the huge grin that spread across his face that he'd read her message and he silently mouthed at her, the words, yes please.

Sarah began. 'We usually eat custard with something like pudding and tarts, but rarely on its own. However, we'll be doing that today so we can judge the merits of the custard alone,' she said and placed spoons next to the sample bowls. 'Up until around ten years ago we only had tinned custard or the dry powder to make your own but now all the supermarkets have their own custard recipe freshly made in tubs.'

Margaret said, 'Oh yes, I always made up my own Birds custard with milk and water. The lads loved it when they were little.'

Olga nodded her head. 'And the thing is with making your own is that you could make it as thin or as thick as you wanted.'

'That's right,' Sarah said. 'Custard is a personal preference, but we usually aim for a medium consistency that will suit all tastes. Also, now-a-days vanilla essence is often added to lift the flavour profile which is another like or dislike but once again we aim for a mid-point. So, if you just comment and score as usual it'll give us a guide to customer preference.'

The taste panel started, and she spent the time wondering what to wear on her date with Mark. She hoped there would be time to shop for a new outfit. Thinking about the clothes hanging in her wardrobe she remembered occasions in London when she'd worn them. The clothes all had certain memories attached to them.

She frowned knowing she didn't want to meet Mark thinking of the past. She wanted this to be a fresh start and a new chapter in her life.

He looked up at her and she melted under his gaze longing to be alone with him. Handing over his form she took it and while the others still had their heads down, she read his reply, 'Saturday at 7.30 outside?' Smiling she nodded her agreement and he happily grinned back.

***

On Saturday night Christine sat on the corner of Sarah's leather sleigh-bed sipping wine while she pulled her new black dress over her head.

'Is it okay?' Sarah asked wriggling the dress down over her slim hips.

The dress was plain black crepe in a sleeveless classic style and ended two inches above her knee.

Christine whistled threw her teeth like they had done at school. 'It's fab!' She said, 'And a perfect fit. You'd think it had been made just for your figure.'

'It's not too short?' Sarah asked. 'I want to look trendy and show my legs off, but I don't want to look like a slapper in a mini dress!'

Christine giggled. 'As if you could ever look like a slapper? Look, it's simple, yet chic and just the right thing to impress him.'

'Thanks for coming over I feel like a nervous teenager again which is ridiculous considering I'm thirty-seven in January,' Sarah said and hugged her.

'No problem,' Christine said getting ready to leave. 'Whenever there's a glass of wine going spare, I'm never far away. And stop worrying; you'll have a great night. The worst thing that can happen is that you don't fancy him, and he ends up a good friend.'

With the knock-em-dead advice from Christine buzzing around in her mind Sarah slipped her feet into black patent stilettos, grabbed her clutch bag, and left in a taxi to the Indian restaurant.

***

In the back of the art studio Ellen pleaded with Mark. 'But you can't wear that blue shirt with the brown trousers!'

She'd made him bring his trousers from the dry cleaners to show her the colour and style then he had explained his choice of shirts to wear. He'd had his hair and beard trimmed and was in a total frenzy about meeting Sarah later that night.

'Well, I can't see why the blue shirt won't go?' he said and tugged on his ear. 'I love that shirt it's really comfortable and easy to wear.'

'Exactly!' Ellen retorted.

He saw her take a deep breath and knew she was trying not to lose her patience. 'But we don't want to look cosy and comfortable tonight, Pop's. We want to look sharp, upbeat and like we've tried to impress the lady, right? Cosy shirts are great for lying around at home but not for a dinner date in a restaurant!'

'Humph,' he muttered but knew she was probably right. 'Okay, I'll wear the cream shirt then and feel like scratching my arms to bits.'

Ellen giggled. 'Oh, by the sound of it, I think you'll have more things on your mind than itchy sleeves on a shirt.'

Grabbing the dry-cleaning bag, he switched off the lights, turned on the alarm and they hurried through the doors and onto the street. With final instructions to relax and enjoy himself, Ellen hurried off and he jumped into his car heading for home to hit the shower.

Just before seven thirty he walked down Cleveland Road towards the restaurant wriggling his arm against his jacket sleeve and trying not to scratch. He wished he hadn't listened to Ellen and worn his old blue shirt. When he neared the restaurant doors, he saw a taxi pull up at the kerbside. Two slim tanned legs in black heeled shoes slid gracefully out of the back seat and he gaped at the woman.

Good, God, he muttered, it was Sarah and she looked absolutely stunning in a short black dress. He blessed Ellen for her advice and automatically pulled his shoulders back with pride. This was his date for the next few hours, and he felt honoured just to be seen out with her.

Quietly, he called her name, 'Sarah?'

She spun around and smiled. 'Oh, hello, Mark,' she said.

He took her hand and gabbled nonsense about walking down from the car park and how he should have offered to pick her up as they stepped inside the restaurant.

A waiter took them to a quiet table in the corner with subdued lights and lit a candle in a bell-shaped glass then took Sarah's jacket. She stood for a few moments before the waiter pulled the leather high-backed chair out and when Mark looked into her gentle blue eyes, he thought his chest would burst with happiness.

'This menu looks delicious with some new dishes that I've never seen before,' she said. 'I love Indian food, but in the past, I've been criticised for staying with the old tired and tested.'

'Me, too,' he said. 'Maybe it's time for us both to start again and try something new?'

He took her hand and squeezed it hoping she understood the double meaning and when the waiter arrived with their drinks, and she ordered one of the chef's special with guineafowl he knew she had.

They started to talk about everything and anything both relaxing easily into each other's company. He told her all about his life with Jessie and the truth about his sham of a marriage and the miscarriages.

'I can see that admitting this has shaken you,' she said. She reached for his hand and covered it with hers.

Sarah smiled. 'And, if you've been brave enough to tell me about your marriage, I'll tell you all about Paul,' she said. 'Well, he'd been good looking, successful, clever, and I'd thought him simply perfect in every way.'

He saw her eyes fill with tears. 'When I found out he'd been cheating I was absolutely devastated. It took me months to even start trying to get over him.'

Mark took her hand and squeezed it in return. His heart filled with love for her and what she'd been through. He wanted to wipe away all her sadness and upsetting memories, but knew, of course, as with himself, this wasn't possible.

Before they realised, they were the only people left in the restaurant and the waiter was hovering near the table.

Mark didn't want the night to end and wanted to stay close to her forever which he knew was ridiculous at such an early stage. 'Can I drop you off?' he asked. 'Or shall I call you a taxi?' Sarah smiled at him and accepted the lift home.

***

Mark looked gorgeous and sexy, and she couldn't think of any more words to describe him because he was with her and grinning like the proverbial Cheshire cat. She knew he was enjoying being with her, as she was with him. Sitting next to him in the car, Sarah decided she even loved the sound of his name.

Her heart pumped with excitement at his closeness, and she clasped her hands fighting the urge to reach out and touch him. Smiling to herself, she decided Christine was about to be proven wrong because boy-oh-boy did she fancy him.

When they pulled up outside her town house, she didn't want to say goodnight. She wanted to continue talking but was unsure because they were together on a first date.

He was older than her and held old-fashioned beliefs and values, which was one of the things she loved about him. What would he think if she asked him to come inside with the usual pun of having coffee? And, although she was convinced that he would be the perfect gentleman and wouldn't pull any fast moves she was still a little hesitant.

'I'm a little out of practise with this bit,' he said turning to face her.

She realised he seemed as desperate to do the right thing as she was and giggled. 'I was just thinking the same thing myself.'

Tenderly he touched her cheek and stared into her eyes.
'How about this then?' He asked and slowly lowered his
lips onto hers.

Chapter Fourteen – Thursday 6th December

The kiss had been gentle at first with his goatee beard tickling her chin but when she'd responded it had become more urgent with hidden strength. It had seemed to last forever.

The next day during Sunday lunch her mam had told her that she had her head in the clouds and Sarah dreamily laughed then agreed with her.

Her dad had said, 'Aye, but isn't that a lovely place to be after all the months of misery and upset you've been through.'

She'd hugged him tight loving the familiar smell of Old Spice aftershave on his home-knitted cardigan.

That kiss hadn't been the only one they'd shared since the dinner date because they had been to the cinema and Mark had sat for two hours with his arm draped along her shoulders. When the credits rolled at the end of the film, he'd kissed her again.

It was what she thought of as grown-up kissing, it wasn't open mouthed, immature, got to get you into bed kissing. It was slow, lingering and we've got all the time in the world kissing. And because they'd both agreed not to rush into this new relationship and take it a gentle pace, she loved it.

***

On Thursday evening at six, she struggled up the stairs to the taste panel room with two heavy bags weighing her down. There were three Christmas cakes in each bag and just when she reached the door Mark bounded up the stairs behind her.

'Hey, wait up. You'll do yourself a mischief lugging them up the stairs,' he cried and took the bags from her while she found the key.

Smiling she followed him through to the kitchen chatting about the film on Wednesday evening and how they'd both loved the special effects. While he lifted the cakes out of the bags, she looked at him from the corner of her eye. The sight of his familiar face gave her a warm feeling which spread right through her body.

He began to tease her, and she playfully chased him out of the kitchen before opening the cakes and choosing the sample numbers for each one.

Jason, Ayesha, Olga, and Margaret arrived and gathered around the table while Sarah remained in the kitchen cutting slices from each cake.

The door opened again, and she looked up in surprise to see Rebecca enter the room. She listened to Rebecca explaining that she wouldn't be staying but wanted to call and thank everyone for the flowers and card. Margaret commiserated with her, and Ayesha thanked her for the support group information.

Mark stood up and guided Rebecca across the room towards the hatch and Sarah waved in greeting.

Quietly, but still within Sarah's earshot, he asked Rebecca, 'How did you get on with everything? I do hope you made peace with your mam before the end?'

Rebecca patted his arm, but Sarah noticed it was in a friendly manner.

'Yes thanks, Mark, I did,' Rebecca said. 'We talked it all through about the adoption and how she couldn't fall pregnant. And why she never told me. I forgave her because I can relate to being the same myself. It's such a sad coincidence that neither of us could have children. Life can be strange, even cruel sometimes.'

Mark nodded. 'It certainly can. But I'm so pleased you managed to talk it through. It'll really help in years to come. Is there any news from the adoption register?'

'Actually, I got a letter today to say my birth mother has agreed to be contacted and the intermediary service will send me through her details then begin preliminary contact between us,' she said. 'So, it's a bit scary but exciting all at the same time.'

'Hey, that's great news,' he said putting his arms around her in a big hug.

Seeing Mark with his arms around another woman made Sarah take a deep breath and feelings of jealousy rumbled deep in the pit of her stomach. She needn't have worried though because his next sentence made her smile with happiness.

'And I just wanted to let you know, Rebecca that I've started to see Sarah on a personal basis. Other than here of course,' he said grinning at both women.

Rebecca poked her head through the hatch and genuinely wished them both all the happiness in the world.

While Sarah put plates of Christmas cake down the centre of the table Rebecca moved towards the door, told them she hoped to come back next week and left the room to everyone's well wishes.

'Oh, what a lovely Christmas smell from the cake,' Margaret said. 'Shall I make a pot of tea to have with it?'

Sarah smiled. 'Can we leave the tea until later, please, Margaret? I know it's tempting but it might mask the judgement and results of the actual cake. If you feel the cake samples are dry to swallow then please drink the water in between to rinse your palette,' she said.

Margaret nodded in understanding.

Sarah said, 'I do agree with the comment about the smell, though. I went out to the supplier's factory in June to watch the cakes being made and it was amazing. They are baked in what they call long travelling ovens which take two hours for the cake to pass through. And, as soon as you enter the huge production area the smell is out of this world!'

Jason grinned. 'Oh, so you go out to see the products being made as well?'

Sarah smiled. 'Yep, visiting and checking supplier sites is all part of my technologist's role,' she said.

Olga nodded with interest. 'It sounds like a great profession. I would have loved an interesting job like that when I was younger but there weren't opportunities for women back then,' she said.

Margaret nodded in agreement and told them all how she'd worked in the abattoir in an unskilled job for most of her life.

Sarah smiled. 'Well, yes, it is a good job,' she said. 'And I'd say, if you are interested in food, have a flair for design and development, and want to work long and hard I certainly would recommend it. Seeing new products that you've worked with on the supermarket shelves is a buzz that never leaves you. And fifteen years later I'm still extraordinarily proud of my achievements.'

Jason said, 'Hmm, I'll keep you in mind when my two girls are thinking of careers.'

'So,' Sarah said. 'Just to double check again with you all, there are nuts and alcohol in the cakes if anyone has allergies?'

'Unfortunately, I've never been allergic to any type of alcohol,' Mark said laughing and Margaret tittered.

While everyone sat in silence completing the sensory forms the quietness of the room was suddenly shattered as the door was opened and flung back against the wall.

An Indian man in his late forties wearing a long grey tunic, and black pantaloons stood on the threshold. Sarah guessed he had to be a relative of Ayesha's because he had the same huge eyes. Sarah heard Ayesha give an audible gasp of shock.

Everyone jerked their heads up in surprise and Sarah said, 'Are you, Mr Verma? Please do come in.'

The man's face contorted with anger and Sarah saw his eyes wildly looking around the room as he advanced towards them all. 'Yes, I am Mr Verma,' he said looking from one to another around the table.

His glare found and settled upon Jason. 'And you! You just stay away from my daughter,' he bellowed. 'I know all about you! You dirty little queer, hiding behind your wife and kids while you run around gay bars defiling yourself!'

Jason's face drained of all colour. He visibly sank into his chair and Sarah could see him begin to tremble.

Mark stood up and said, 'Now, look here…'

Mr Verma took no notice. 'And if you don't stop filling Ayesha's head full of rubbish, I'll speak to your wife,' he shouted then suddenly lunged across the end of the table and punched Jason squarely in the face.

Jason fell backwards off his chair with the force of the blow.

Mark jumped up and grabbed the back of Mr Verma's tunic holding him steady so he couldn't strike again.

Margaret screamed with fright.

Olga rushed to Jason and knelt beside him then demanded ice for his face, and Sarah jumped up then ran into the kitchen.

Ayesha started to shout at her father in Hindu. Mr Verma yanked himself free from Marks grasp and turned towards Ayesha. He grabbed her arm to drag her out of the room and she burst into tears looking at him with abject terror in her eyes.

Margaret cried out, 'No, no, don't hurt her!'

Mark stood in front of the doorway and put a hand up in front of Mr Verma's sweating face. 'Now, let's just calm down,' he said firmly. 'I think it would be best if you go home and cool down. Ayesha can stay here with us until you've got control of yourself. We'll bring her home later.'

An uneasy silence hung in the room while Mr Verma breathed heavily in and out looking at everyone's faces. His shoulders sank in defeat at Marks words and removing his hold on Ayesha he ran a hand through his dishevelled hair.

Jason, helped up onto his feet by Olga and holding a bag of ice to his eye slowly walked around the table and stood shoulder to shoulder with Mark.

Mr Verma stormed out of the room and Mark quietly closed the door shut behind him.

Margaret ran and put her arms around Ayesha who burst into uncontrollable sobbing. Jason clapped Mark on the back and said, 'You're our blooming hero!'

Olga helped Sarah upright the two chairs and pick up the paper plates and cake that had been knocked to the floor.

Margaret sat Ayesha down onto a chair and cuddled her while she apologised repeatedly for her father's behaviour.

'B…but how did he know I was here?' Ayesha wailed while Margaret wiped the tears from her face.

Jason slumped down onto a chair and Olga inspected his eye. 'You're going to have a bonny shiner in the morning, alright,' she said.

Jason gave her a lop-sided grin. 'Thanks for helping me, Olga,' he said.

Sarah tried to bring order to the chaos. 'Oh, dear, I've never had anything happen like this before, but I suppose you have been assaulted on our premises,' she said. 'Would you like me to call the police and report the incident?'

Mark put his arm around Sarah. 'It's okay,' he said in his calm and comforting manner. 'It was nobody's fault as such.'

Ayesha jumped up. 'It was. It was my fault! He must have been following me all the time and I didn't know,' she cried looking beseechingly at Jason. 'Honestly, I'm terribly sorry, Jason.'

Jason took her hand when she stood forlornly in front of him. 'Look, it's not your fault that your father is a bully. I'm fine, really, I've had worse than this off my brothers,' he said giving her a wobbly smile.

'And all those horrible things he called you?' Ayesha said hanging her head. 'I'm so sorry. I don't know where that's come from? Maybe he followed us into the pub that night after the support group.'

Sarah nodded her head at Mark who smiled in understanding. Olga looked from one to another and raised an eyebrow.

Suddenly, Ayesha took her bag and jacket from the chair then ran out of the room.

'Leave her to me, I'll make sure she's okay,' Margaret said and grabbed her anorak then hurried after her.

Mark offered to drive Jason and Olga home while Sarah threw all the sample cakes into a black rubbish bag.

Before they left the room he whispered in her ear, 'I'll ring you later tonight.'

***

While Sarah wearily turned the key in her front door, she remembered she hadn't given everyone their vouchers and made a mental note to hand out double the following week. The upset had worn her out and her mind buzzed with all the happenings.

She felt so sorry for Ayesha and couldn't imagine how it must feel to live in fear of your father. She smiled thinking of her own gentle Dad and decided to call on Sunday morning where she'd find him pottering in his garden shed.

He'd never once lifted a hand in temper when she and Hollie were growing up even though his patience must have been tested to the limit. Especially when they were awkward teenagers.

She wondered if Ayesha was close to her mother and why Mrs Verma didn't protect her daughter? She knew that her mam didn't always agree with everything she and Hollie did but would fight to the death to safeguard either of them.

Stripping off her clothes she stood under a steaming hot shower and thought of Jason and how her original impression was right. But there lay another mystery, she thought. Why would he be married with two young babies? And, out of everyone in the room she couldn't believe it had been Olga who had gone to help Jason. They were usually at loggerheads with each other.

Wrapped in a soft white bathrobe she plodded back through to the lounge, booted up her laptop and decided when Mark rang later, she would ask his opinion of the events.

She twirled the wire from the mouse around her fingers and dreamily thought of Mark. She remembered Jason calling him their hero because that's just what he was. Her hero.

He'd been strong and steadfast holding onto Mr Verma then afterwards firmly resolute. So much so, that the Indian man knew his bullying wouldn't be tolerated. And when he'd stood in the doorway to prevent him dragging poor Ayesha out of the door, she'd felt like swooning into his capable arms.

Glancing into her email inbox her eyes immediately snapped open in shock at the familiar email address. It was Paul's.

Gingerly she clicked the email open and read:
From paul.davies to sarah.williams
Hi Sarah, I know this email will be a shock after all this time, but I can't stop thinking about you and all the happy

years we were together. I know now, that by leaving you, I have made the biggest mistake of my life and I still love you. Is there the slightest chance that you could forgive me and take me back?

  Paul XX

Chapter Fifteen – Thursday 13th December

Sarah sent Paul a reply saying she was on holiday and would answer the following week. She was stalling for time because her mind was in complete turmoil with the admission that he still loved her.

Mark had asked her out for a drink over the weekend, but she declined using a migraine for an excuse. She had some serious thinking to do. It wasn't that she didn't want to see Mark, but she desperately wanted a clear head to try and sort her feelings out.

Christine was away with friends, but she told her about Paul's email on her mobile.

'The cheek of him!' Christine cried. 'Who the hell does he think he is?'

'I know, it's scandalous,' she replied. 'But if this had happened a couple of months ago, I'd have been delighted to hear from him again.'

'OMG, Sarah,' she said. 'He's a lying creep and he tore your life apart. Surely you can't be giving the idea any serious thought?'

Sarah choked back a huge lump in her throat. 'W…well, I was in love with him for such a long time and I'd be telling lies if I said I'd stopped thinking about him all together.'

She ended the call promising Christine she wouldn't make any decisions until she got home, and they had the time to talk it through properly. Sarah spent the weekend thinking of Paul and their life together in London. Their fabulous apartment and great friends, the buzz of life in the capital, the parties, and theatres they loved to visit. And how perfect it had all been. She still missed it and tried not to think that she was now living her life in second-best mode in North Shields.

On the following Thursday evening she stood in the kitchen cutting up sausage rolls into bite-size pieces when Mark put his head through the hatch.

'Hey, there, how's the head?' he asked looking genuinely concerned. 'I've missed you.'

She smiled. 'Hey, yourself,' she said. 'And as I told you on the texts, its loads better, thanks.'

'Hmm,' he replied.

Sarah could tell by the look on his face that he wasn't entirely convinced.

'Everyone, except Ayesha is here now,' he said and picked up two sample plates to take to the table.

She followed him into the room with the remainder and greeted everyone.

'You look pale today, Sarah?' Margaret said.

Mark told them how she'd suffered with migraine all weekend. She felt uncomfortable especially about the lie she had told him and tried to shift the attention away from herself.

Sarah asked. 'Is Ayesha not coming this week?'

Olga's eyes were wide with curiosity and said, 'I wonder if she's run away?'

'Well, it wouldn't surprise me if she had,' Jason said. 'She's so scared of her bully of a father.'

Sarah looked at Jason. His face was drawn, and his eye socket was still puffed up, the eyelid was blue and black in the corner. Olga had been right Mr Verma's fist had certainly left him with a real shiner.

'Oh, I wouldn't think so,' Margaret said. 'I'm sure she'll be fine.'

Jason and Olga stared at Margaret and Sarah could tell they thought the same. Margaret had a smug look of satisfaction on her face as though she seemed to know more about Ayesha than she was saying.

Sarah tried to change the conversation and looked at Rebecca then smiled. 'Good to see you back, Rebecca. Maybe you couldn't resist the temptation of sausage rolls, eh?'

Rebecca smiled and shook her long hair which she wore loose with only a light touch of make-up on her face. Her shoulders were drooped, and she sat with her hands in her lap. Sarah thought she looked quite vulnerable. Her usual self-important swagger was long gone, and, she decided, from a woman's point of view, this toned-down version of Rebecca was much more attractive.

A baby's wailing cry was heard on the other side of the door.

Jason looked up suddenly and cried out. 'That's one of the girls!'

The door opened and Stacey stood there gripping the handle of a double buggy. She edged the buggy forward while Jason ran around the table towards her. 'It's too wide to come through the door,' he explained.

She glared at him and snarled. 'Tell me something I don't know.'

His shoulders sank. 'What are you doing here?'

Stacey put the break on the buggy with her foot and stepped into the room. She shouted, 'Come on, then, which one of you is it?'

Everyone looked at each other in silence and puzzlement.

Sarah stared at Stacey. 'What do you mean?' she asked. 'We are just starting the panel but if you want to come in and wait?'

'I'm his wife!' Stacey shouted. 'I'm not waiting around while one of you lot gets her claws in to him.'

Sarah still couldn't understand what she meant and looked dumfounded. She raised her hands up in defeat. 'I'm sorry, but I really have no idea what you are talking about?'

Jason approached Stacey. 'Look, just leave it. You're making a fool of yourself, let's go home.'

Stacey rounded on him. 'I'm not leaving until I find out which one of them you are having an affair with, and who is responsible for giving you the black eye,' she yelled. 'It can't be Sarah because you said she was seeing Mark, so which other one is it?'

Sarah gasped and she heard Mark do the same.

Olga raised herself up in her chair. 'My dear, I hardly think this is the time or the place, we are all just friends here.'

Stacey looked up the table towards her and then spotted Rebecca. 'It's you, isn't it?' she shrieked. 'Fancy a young toy-boy, did you? And maybe your husband found out and gave him the black eye?'

Rebecca's face crumbled, and Sarah could see the temper flare in Mark's eyes.

Sarah gently shook her head at him then stood up to face Stacey. As much as she didn't want to get involved with their outside lives she couldn't stand by and see Rebecca wrongly accused in a defenceless state.

'Stacey, this is my taste panel session to which you are not invited. Rebecca is not having an affair with your husband she has just buried her mother last week. And there is no one here, not that I am aware of, that is having an affair with Jason,' she said firmly. 'Now I would be grateful if you would leave the room so that I can get on with my work.'

'You, tramp!' Stacey hissed and opened her mouth to continue but Jason grabbed the sleeve of her denim jacket and pulled her towards the door.

'It's none of these women,' he yelled at her. 'It's a guy that works in the pub that I've been seeing!'

The babies started to howl with the sound of Jason's angry voice.

Margaret gasped in distress.

Jason grabbed his satchel from the back of the chair and with Stacey staring at him incredulously he forcibly pulled her though the door and closed it shut behind him.

Olga exclaimed, 'Well, really!'

Rebecca looked at Olga and began to giggle uncontrollably.

Sarah slumped down into her seat and looked around the table at everyone. 'Sausage roll, anyone?' she said.

Everyone, even Olga, burst out laughing.

They all tasted the samples, and the merits of pork sausage-meat were discussed with Olga and Margaret holding different opinions about the texture of the pastry. The results of the panels were varied but all agreed that personal preference played a great part in the expectations of a sausage roll.

When Olga, Margaret and Rebecca had collected their vouchers and left the room, Mark took hold of Sarah's hand.

'Don't know about you but I could do with a glass of wine?'

She knew it was only fair to offer him an explanation. He certainly deserved honesty from her if nothing else. 'Yeah, I could do with one myself,' she said, and they left together heading for the pub.

***

Settling into a corner seat in the busy pub she slipped her jacket off and looked at Mark's back standing at the bar. They were broad solid shoulders unlike Paul's young thin shoulders, and she cursed herself for making such comparisons. It wasn't fair to do that to Mark because they were in effect, two entirely different men. She was attracted to Mark but in such a contrasting way to Paul that she was struggling to sort it out. But she knew it was only fair to decide about Paul by her feelings for him alone.

She'd told Mark on their first date together that Paul was good-looking but that had been an understatement. Paul was the type of guy that when he walked into a room every woman stopped what they were doing simply to stare at him. His eyes were deep sparkling blue and under lights they could even look turquoise. They were fringed by the longest eyelashes she'd ever seen on a man. Smiling, she remembered the first time she had looked at him and gasped in wonder. She'd never thought for one moment he would be interested in her and had been astonished when he'd asked her out on a date.

She looked up to see Mark walking towards the table carrying glasses of wine and smiled. 'Oh, lovely, thanks. I'm ready for this,' she said taking a large mouthful. She felt the cool white wine slide easily down her throat and a calming sensation flood through her.

'Yeah, that's two weeks running we've had upset in the room,' he said. 'But I suppose with such diverse characters clumped together there were bound to be some antics.'

She giggled saying, 'Antics? That's a word my dad would use.'

'Well, I suppose escapades is probably a better word. And Jason certainly sounds as though he's been having plenty of them!'

She told him about her first impressions of Jason on week one and how she'd chastised herself for making assumptions about a person by looks alone.

He nodded. 'But it's certainly not fair on Stacey if she didn't know, of course. And by the look of dire shock on her face it was as much of a revelation to her as it was to all of us.'

'Yeah, it's certainly a massive secret to keep from your partner,' she said nodding. 'And I feel bad now for speaking so harshly to her, but when she started accusing Rebecca I lost my temper, I'm afraid.'

'Hmm,' he pondered raising an eyebrow. 'Secrets are not good things to keep in close relationships.'

She knew this was another comment with a double meaning and felt uneasy with the thought of explaining about Paul. She could of course not tell him and make up an excuse but when she saw the sincerity in his eyes, she knew only the truth would do.

She saw him chew on his bottom lip then he said, 'Look, I know there's something wrong with you, and although I've no reason not to believe you had a migraine at the weekend, but you look pale and tired as your mind is somewhere else completely. So, to use another saying, a problem shared, is a problem halved?'

Sarah sighed and licked her lips. 'Okay, I'm going to tell you what's happened because you deserve to know the truth and I can't make up excuses or tell you lies,' she said taking a deep breath. 'My, ex, Paul, has sent me an email last Friday saying he still loves me and wants us to go back to London together.'

Although she knew she was doing the right thing she hadn't been prepared for the look on his face - he looked crestfallen.

An awkward silence descended between them as he lowered his eyes and began to fiddle with a beer mat. She felt terrible. She could tell by his face that she'd hurt him, and she took another two large gulps of wine wondering if she should continue explaining.

He raised his head and gave her a little smile. 'Well, I wasn't sure what to expect but it certainly wasn't that! No wonder you didn't want to meet me at the weekend,' he said. 'But I do thank you for at least being honest.'

Feeling the last few days of stress and anxiety build up inside her she stuttered, 'I…I'm sorry, maybe I should have tried to say it differently, but I'm totally shocked after six months of hearing nothing from him. I just can't seem to get my head around it?'

He touched her arm gently. 'So, I've lost you after two dates,' he said and looked into her eyes. 'You've no doubt decided to give it another go with him?'

'Oooh, hell, I don't know,' she wailed. 'I don't know what to do or think.'

She drained the glass of wine feeling her eyes prick with tears. For one split second she wanted to throw herself into Mark's broad chest and feel his strong arms holding her tight.

Suddenly, they both looked up at the sound of Jason's voice and saw him fast approaching the table. 'Hiya, what a stroke of luck to find you both in here,' he said and straddled a stool on the other side of the table.

Sarah instantly choked back her tears, lifted her shoulders, and tried to pull herself together. Mark shuffled uneasily on his seat and drained his glass of red wine.

Jason grinned. 'And I can see I'm just in time to get you both another drink,' he said jumping back up from the stool.

Mark stood up too. 'No, it's fine. I can get them.'

But Jason wouldn't listen and headed off to the bar.

'Did you want another glass?' he asked her quietly. 'Because if you don't, I can sit and listen to him if you wanted to head off home?'

He can't wait to get rid of me, she thought and bit her lip. And who could blame him. But the thought of going home alone with the incessant turmoil in her head would be worse than staying. 'Thanks, I probably don't deserve such kindness,' she said. 'But I could do with another, so, I'll stay for one more.'

They both looked ahead watching Jason flirt with the barman. For the first time she felt uneasy sitting next to Mark. Wanting to break the silence, she asked, 'I wonder if that's him? The guy he's been having an affair with?'

'Well, it certainly looks like it,' Mark said. 'There are definitely hot vibes and a real buzz between them.'

Jason carried a tray with the three glasses over to the table. 'I'm so pleased you are both here because I seriously need to apologise for Stacey's outburst earlier,' he said. 'You see, it was all my own fault.'

Sarah sipped her wine slowly. 'It's okay, Jason,' she said.

'No, it's not. Stacey should never have barged into the room like that telling everyone that you two were an item,' he said. 'It was out of order and if you were trying to keep it a secret, I'm terribly sorry.'

Mark interrupted. 'There's nothing to keep secret,' he said and patted her arm. 'Sarah and I are simply good friends and have loads in common like, Indian food and James Bond movies.'

She nodded her head and smiled at Mark in gratitude for getting them out of an embarrassing situation.

She turned her smile onto Jason in the hope of making him feel easier.

'Aah, that's great,' Jason said. 'I don't feel so bad now. I'd hate to upset either of you because you've been such good friends over the last nine weeks.'

They all nodded in understanding while Jason went on to explain how he'd been fighting with himself for years over his sexuality. How he had met and had to marry Stacey. And how coming out was going to cause such an upset with his family.

Mark said, 'But surely you must have realised by coming in here and having an affair on your own doorstep, you would get found out sooner or later?'

'I know and that was wrong of me,' Jason said. 'But I didn't expect to fall for him so quickly or deeply. You've no idea how hard I tried not to set foot into this pub after I'd first met him. And, I just thought I'd have one date with him to see what it was like.'

'Hmm,' Mark muttered, 'It's easily done I suppose. Instant attraction can be the devil itself.'

Sarah looked into Mark's eyes and could feel his pain and upset. How could she have done this to him, she thought, after everything he'd been through with Jessie. But she hadn't meant to hurt him. And in her own way, she felt just as wretched.

Jason said, 'So, when me and Stacey got back home, I told her the truth from start to finish and she went crazy. She's threatening to take the babies and go back up to live in Scotland with her parents. I lost it and had to get out before I did something to regret. I wanted to come and warn my fella that all hell is about to break loose,' he said nodding his head over towards the bar.

Sarah was amazed. 'And you're going to run the risk of losing your family altogether for him?'

Jason looked across at her and simpered. 'I'm not sure what's going to happen. Stacey will have rung the troops up in Scotland by now and they'll all be on their way down to sort me out I suppose.'

'Well, at the risk of sounding like a boring old man,' Mark said. 'You've got an awful lot of thinking to do. Two beautiful young daughters are a hell of a sacrifice to make for someone you've known for a few weeks.'

Sarah agreed nodding her head as Mark pulled on his jacket. 'Well, I'd better get going. Sam will be waiting for his dinner,' he said. 'Good night and see you both next week.'

Chapter Sixteen – Saturday 15ᵗʰ December

On Saturday morning after an extra-long lie in bed and feeling refreshed from an extremely busy week at work, Sarah emailed Paul.

From sarah.williams to paul.davies

Hi, Paul, yes, this email is a total shock. I've wrestled with myself for days now as to whether I should even answer it but here I am. I suppose nine years is a long time to be together and I do still think about us together. Especially at this time of year as it was always such a special time. I'm not going to do chit chat, I'll just plunge straight in. No matter how much I loved you, and boy oh boy did I love you, I don't think I'd ever be able to trust you again. When all the details of your affair materialised, the hardest thing for me to understand was how you could have lied to me for five months to see her behind my back. How, if at all, do I get through that?

Sarah

Deciding it was the best she could write she pressed the send button before she had time to change her mind. Heading towards the shower, she remembered Christine's advice to answer the email with only two choice words, get lost, but she couldn't do that. Whichever way this communication went, if nothing else, she wanted what was known as some type of closure.

She dressed carefully in flat-heeled, knee-high boots for a Christmas shopping trip into Newcastle with Christine. Overnight the temperatures had dropped and when she looked out of the window, she saw a thick white frost covering the footpaths and roof tops.

Rather than driving into the city centre they intended to take the metro and she chose a short denim skirt, thick ribbed tights, and a blue polo neck jumper to complete her outfit. Because she wore suits for work all week, she liked to look casual at weekends.

Before leaving the house, she checked her inbox and was amazed to see Paul had replied so quickly.

paul. davies to sarah.williams

Thanks so much for answering, Sarah, I know it's much more than I deserve. It wouldn't be easy for us to move forward and leave the past behind but if there is a likelihood that you would consider trying again, I can promise you wholeheartedly I will never ever tell another lie as long as I live. I'll work so hard at building your trust up again if only you could find a way to forgive me? I was so stupid to have my head turned by a promise of a glamorous Italian lifestyle that to be frank, living here now leaves me cold. The warmest days of my life were with you in our apartment in Camden. I wonder if Dad might rent it back to us. Just one word from you and I'll pack up here and be back in London on the next flight. I miss YOU and our old life together so much.

I love you heaps,

Paul.

XXXXXX

Digesting the words, she sighed heavily then wrapped a blue cashmere scarf around her neck. She would reply later, she decided and pulled on her jacket then hurried out of the door.

***

Christine was standing at the doors to the metro station waiting for her and had bought them both tickets. Dressed in a brown, suede jacket and jeans and with her hair pushed into a bakers-boy cap she grinned excitedly at Sarah. They sat together on the train and while they chattered during the journey, she looked at her friend feeling the usual comfortable contentment. It was the same feeling of love she had with her family and knew that no matter what happened between them nothing would ever mar their friendship. It was effortless.

After three hours buying gifts, they looked at the traditional Christmas display in Fenwick's department store window. Giggling and singing along to the carols they declared themselves well and truly in the festive spirit but hungry and made their way inside the store to the restaurant.

Dropping down gratefully onto chairs and placing all the carrier bags under the table they ordered lunch straight away. Fenwick's made the best chicken Caesar salad in town and because Sarah worked with food, she was willing to pay a little extra for decent quality produce.

This fact however, meant nothing to Christine because she had no interest in food whatsoever. She was the type of person who only ate to live and would happily eat beans on toast three times a day with no thought to her diet.

'Christmas shopping is exhausting, my feet are killing me,' Christine exclaimed taking a gulp of white wine.

Sarah giggled and glanced around the room with beautiful gold decorations hanging from the ceiling and the large glittering Christmas tree in the corner. Waiters dressed in black trousers with white shirts hurried between tables carrying plates of food and a general buzz of festive cheer

Christine raised an eyebrow at Sarah. 'So, when are you going to tell me about it?'

Sarah took a deep breath then told her word for word what Paul's email had said.

'Hmph!' Christine grunted. 'And what's your reply going to be?'

Sarah put her head down and wavered. 'I'm not completely decided. I think it's harder because of the time of the year,' she said and waited for a blast of derisory comments.

Christine sighed. 'Look, Sarah, Christmas is lovely. It's cute and a cuddly time of year. But it only lasts two weeks,' she said. 'How are you going to get through the other fifty weeks of the year if you can't trust him?'

Sarah shrugged. 'I keep thinking of all the Christmas parties we went to with our friends and the beautiful apartment we had with our fabulous tree in the hall. And I could probably tell you every present he has bought me over the nine years.'

She opened her leather purse, took out a small photograph of Paul and her standing in front of the tree and placed it on the table in front of Christine. 'He is so gorgeous and when I remember how we made love to each other,' she said feeling her cheeks flush at the memories.

Christine looked at the photograph and then lifted her head. 'Sarah, you know how much I love you, honey. You're like the sister I never had and although I'd like to coo along and agree with everything you've said, I simply can't!'

Sarah shuffled uncomfortably in the chair and sipped her wine. 'It's okay, I know you're looking out for me the same way I would do for you.'

'Good, well, here goes,' she said. 'Your great London friends have practically forgotten you now and two of them knew he was with the model and didn't tell you for five months. That's not what I call being a good friend. The apartment was organised by you, not him. You paid all the bills and kept the budget under control. It was you who hung decorations and dressed the tree. The fabulous gifts he bought you were all on his credit card and I remember on two occasions you had to return them because they were so extravagant, he couldn't afford them. So, while he pranced around looking gorgeous it was you who kept him grounded with his feet on the floor. And, the one present you dreamt of during those nine years, an engagement ring, was never forthcoming. And as much as I'd love to see you happy, Paul just cannot commit to anything!'

The waiter approached with their salads and Christine sat back in the chair taking a deep breath. Sarah felt tearful even though she knew deep down her friend was right. She quickly pushed the photograph back into her purse.

When the waiter left the table Christine squeezed her arm. 'I'm sorry, love, but as our mothers would say, I'm trying to be cruel to be kind, and, you have to open your eyes and smell the coffee?'

Sarah pulled her shoulders back sniffing the tears away. Wanting to change the subject, she said, 'You're right, I know you are. Come-on let's forget about it for now and eat this gorgeous salad. I don't want to spoil our lovely day out together.'

Later when Sarah reached home, she filled the bath with hot water and relaxed back against the roll top edge squeezing her eyes shut. She allowed herself the luxury of remembering the apartment they'd shared on the quiet and leafy, Regents Park side of Camden.

She could imagine the buzz of activity on the high street where she'd gone shopping at the Inverness Street markets for fruit and vegetables. There were great rock bars and restaurants which they'd loved going to, and one called, Fifty-Five, the cocktail bar where she'd met Paul.

Camden was great for transport it was only a short bus ride into Covent Garden in the heart of the city and the northern line for Kings Cross Station when she made visits home.

She knew in her heart that Christine was right to challenge her sentimental memories and this time she had to force her mind to rule her heart because she couldn't go backwards and make the same mistakes again. But relishing in the warm water she remembered her first date with Paul and still tingled with pleasure.

When she had arrived in the cocktail bar, and he'd helped her slither up onto a stool in her short sky-blue sequined dress she'd felt she was living the dream. From the second she arrived he'd made her feel like a princess. He was the most attentive and tactile man she'd ever met. He had stroked her jaw line, twirled a finger through her hair, planted kisses on her cheek, draped an arm around her shoulders, and had never left her side. It was as if he'd been glued to her.

She remembered extricating herself from him to go to the Ladies and when she had walked back into the bar every woman was looking at her with pure envy. She'd wished she could have taken a photograph and put it in her old school for the bullies to see who had called her, fatty Williams.

The water in the bath was cooling now and she sighed wishing she could go with what her heart felt and drown out all Christine's sensible comments. The last and most crucial point, which she hadn't mentioned to Christine, was the fact that Paul had never wanted children. And when they'd first met, she'd decided she wasn't bothered either way. But now she thought differently to what she had back then, and sometimes was feeling broody.

Placing her hand on top of her flat stomach she wondered how it would feel to have a baby growing inside. If she went back to Paul, this would be something she would never know. And, if she told him she wanted a baby how would he react? And more importantly, she thought, would he make a good father.

After pulling on her old tracksuit, Hollie and her niece, Sophia arrived for a quick coffee. Sophia was four years old and excited about Santa coming. It was hard to keep her still in one place. She danced around the lounge in her fairy costume practising for the pantomime and Sarah rolled on the large shag-pile rug then tickled her until they were both giggling hysterically.

'Enough!' Hollie shouted but laughed herself. 'Settle down both of you. We've got another ten days to go yet.'

'Oooh, more, please, Aunty Sarah,' Sophia shrieked.

Sarah loved being called Aunty. It gave her a lovely warm feeling inside and she hugged Sophie tightly inhaling her clean-shampooed hair nuzzled in her neck. But catching the glint in Hollie's eye she lifted her up onto the settee and gave her a mug of orange juice while they sipped their coffee. This is what family is all about, she thought, and sighed contentedly.

She saw Hollie looking at her Christmas tree in the corner of the room.

Hollie said, 'The little Christmas tree is nice. Your silver and blue baubles look great. Bang on trend.'

'Oh, it's okay, I suppose. But I keep remembering our huge tree in the London apartment. I still miss living there sometimes,' she said. 'I loved Camden because there was always so much to do.'

Hollie snorted. 'Well, I hope you're not missing the creep you lived with,' she said. 'And London! You couldn't pay me to live there. It costs a fortune, the streets are dirty, the traffic is noisy, and nobody talks to one another. There's no such thing as friendly neighbours down there.'

Sarah looked at her wondering as sisters, how they could be so different from each other. She'd always thought Hollie had been jealous of her London lifestyle, and said, 'But I thought you liked my place when you came down to visit?'

'Oh, I did. London is a wonderful place for a short break, but I couldn't live there. What will happen in a few years' time when you won't want to go out four or five times a week, and the thought of theatre and clubs is no longer attractive,' she said shaking her head. 'No, I'd rather have my friends and family around me and feel safe and loved than be miles away in a trendy, lonely place. As far as I'm concerned, London is definitely not all it's cracked up to be!'

Sarah sighed with indecision. 'Hmm,' she uttered knowing there was truth in what Hollie had just said.

Later, she stood at the window waving at Hollie and Sophia down the street until they'd turned the corner. She looked out across the river and thought of the old Northeast saying, you can take the lass out of Tyneside, but you'll never take Tyneside out of the lass.

Smiling, she wondered at the age of thirty-two if she'd finally succumbed to this, or had it never actually left her.

Chapter Seventeen – Thursday 20th December

Unbelievably, it was the last taste panel of the year. The Christmas puddings were unwrapped, and the microwaves were set ready in the kitchen with her numbered plates. Collecting bowls from the cupboard, Sarah decided she was glad the sessions were ending for the Christmas holidays. She had so much office work to finish before the holidays it made her head spin.

Her desk was littered with unfinished reports. She had lists of jobs pinned on her board and her diary was still crammed with meetings. She could of course, be like other colleagues and leave work until she returned in January, but this wasn't, and never had been, the way she worked.

Opening the hatch through to the panel room she noted none of the panellists were early this week. Not even Mark had made an appearance, which considering what had happened wasn't surprising. And even though her head had been full of Paul and the decision she had to make; she'd still found herself wondering how Mark was.

By six o'clock the room was still empty. Sarah knew it was the time of year when everyone was busy, and she usually found the last panel was often short on numbers. Three housewives had been missing from her Tuesday night session.

Her mobile rang and she heard Rebecca's voice shouting above the noise of heavy traffic telling her she would be coming but would be late.

The door opened and Olga arrived closely followed by Mark.

She hurried through to greet them. 'Hello, there, I was just wondering how many would actually make it tonight,' she said smiling sheepishly at Mark. 'Rebecca has just rung to say she's running extremely late. I suppose the traffic is bad again tonight?'

Mark nodded. 'It's not good but there again it is the time of year when everyone runs around like headless chickens,' he said.

Olga agreed and while Sarah busied herself with paperwork, she thought back to the first week when she'd watched Mark's lovely grin spread across his face. She realised with a pang how much she was going to miss seeing him.

'It must be a terrible time for you at Christmas without your wife?' Olga asked. 'It's only two years since I lost Philip, and after sharing so many Christmases together, it takes a lot of getting used to being on my own.'

Sarah looked at Olga's face properly for what must be the first time in ten weeks. Because of her challenging personality she'd been guilty of looking at her troublesome demeanour rather than seeing her for the lady she was. She had huge sparkling blue eyes, beautiful smooth skin and Sarah decided she must have been stunning when she was younger.

She listened while Olga told Mark how she'd be spending Christmas Day at the golf club with friends and then the door opened, and Jason hurried inside and sat down next to Mark.

'Hey, there,' Mark said. 'How's it going?'

Jason nodded. 'Okay, well, it's not good, but things are at least out in the open and I feel better than I did. Half of Scotland charged down at the weekend to try and talk sense into me, but I actually came-out,' he said, and looked at the puzzlement on Olga's face. 'It means that I've admitted to everyone that I'm gay.'

Olga sniffed and lowered her head pretending to examine the large emerald ring on her finger.

Ignoring her, Jason continued, 'So, we're all going back up to Scotland tomorrow for the Christmas holiday. It'll give us time to talk and make plans for the future.'

Mark nodded then asked, 'And how did the family take it?'

Jason looked thoughtful. 'Very shocked but on the whole much better than I thought they'd be. Dad is the worst, but mam reckons he'll come around eventually, and my oldest brother told me he'd always known I was different. So, he wasn't as gobsmacked as the others,' he said. 'And I've finished with the guy at the pub.'

Before anyone had time to comment the door opened and Margaret and Ayesha tumbled in together. Sarah was pleased to see Ayesha, and they all greeted her warmly with comments about how well she looked.

'Well, it's all down to my saviour, here,' she said smiling at Margaret who had removed her red anorak and was slipping it around the back of a chair.

Margaret tutted and waved a fluttering hand in dismissal.

Ayesha's eyes were shining when she smiled at everyone around the table and folded her hands calmly in front of her. 'First, may I take a minute of your panel time, Sarah?'

Sarah nodded. 'I think you'll have to we are all in suspense.'

'Well, after my father came here and disgraced me two weeks ago, I went back to Margaret's house with her and basically I haven't left,' she said.

Everyone gaped at them both.

She continued, 'I wanted to run away but Margaret persuaded me to stay the night and she rang my father and told him I was with her and was safe. She also told him that we would contact him the following day when everyone had time to calm down. She let me stay in a lovely blue room with aeroplanes on the walls and I slept for nine hours. I must have been exhausted,' she said. 'Then the following day she went to collect some of my clothes and told my father that she thought it would best if I stayed with her for a while until a resolution to the problem could be found. And yesterday my parents came for tea and Margaret has managed to convince them to postpone the wedding until next summer!'

Mark was first to react and clapped his hands towards Margaret. 'Well done, you,' he said. And then everyone joined in congratulating and cheering until poor Margaret was bright red in the face and totally flustered.

Ayesha laid her head on Margaret shoulder and the older lady put her arm around her.

Jason cried, 'You look just like a grandma and granddaughter.'

Margaret's eyes washed with tears. 'Aah, she's a delight to have in the house and I do love having someone to fuss over. I've told her parents that losing your children is the worst thing that can happen in life, and I should know.'

'Well, that's great,' Olga said kindly. 'Now you'll have someone to eat all those two for one offer's you've been storing up in the pantry.'

Sarah excused herself and headed into the kitchen to cook the puddings in the microwaves. Setting the timer, she thought of Margaret as the dark horse in the group and shook her head in amazement. This quiet, nervous woman who in week one had portrayed the image of a silly old lady too nervous to speak out in the group, had been the mainstay over the last ten weeks.

She'd been a quiet confidant to snobby Olga. She had befriended high and mighty Rebecca and had now taken Ayesha into her home of safety and negotiated with the bully, Mr Verma. And this was all done in the same red anorak and slacks. Emptying the puddings from containers onto plates, she decided, it was what her mam meant when she said that northern women were the strongest in the country.

Carrying the puddings through she placed them down the centre of the table.

'Hmm, what a gorgeous smell,' Ayesha said looking at the puddings. 'I'm looking forward to these.'

Olga started to tell everyone the history of how Christmas puddings were made in the Victorian times and how her mother had always put sixpences into her pudding mix. Margaret laughed with pleasure at the memories and confirmed the story in her own family.

Jason asked, 'It's a wonder that no one broke their teeth?'

Olga smiled. 'Oh no, that didn't happen because we all knew they were there,' she said. 'And if you were lucky enough to get a coin you licked the pudding from it until it was shining silver again and placed it on the edge of your bowl.'

They all started to taste the puddings and complete the forms while Sarah prepared her final talk and spread the last bunch of vouchers onto the table. The results were good for their supermarket which gave everyone a happy buzz and was a close second to the market-leaders Christmas pudding. Sarah was delighted.

'So, here we are at our last panel,' Sarah said smiling at the group. 'I've done a chart of results if anyone wants to take a copy. It tells you which supermarket scored the most winners over the last ten weeks and I'm pleased to say we are in the top three out of a list of nine. Our buyers and marketing guys will be thrilled with these results. As I am because it supports the results we've recorded in our department.'

Olga took a copy saying, 'Oh, that'll be interesting to read.'

Pointing at the front of the chart Sarah explained, 'It starts from week one where we tasted quiche tarts,' she said.

She looked up to see Mark staring at her with such melancholy it made her catch her breath. Was he thinking of that first week when they met and how they'd felt drawn to each other? She looked at his familiar brown eyes through the clear lens of his glasses wishing things could have been different.

'God, that seems like a lifetime away,' Jason murmured. 'So much has happened since then.'

'You're not kidding!' Ayesha said and Margaret patted her hand.

Sarah said, 'And, I just wanted to thank you all for making the effort to come each week. I know because of the unforeseen circumstances that have arisen it's not been an easy time for some of you to attend. And I do appreciate it. I've managed to get my hands on a few more vouchers so there are two for everyone this week as an extra Christmas present. I know you'll all put them to good use.'

Margaret and Ayesha gushed over the kindness and Jason tried to work out how many extra nappies he could buy with them which made everyone laugh.

The door opened and Rebecca stood in the doorway looking dishevelled and traumatised.

Sarah wondered if she had been in a car accident.

Mark turned to look at her and jumped to his feet. 'Rebecca! What's happened?'

Tears were streaming down her face and her mascara had run in two thick black lines down one cheek. In one hand she held a letter and with the back of her other hand she rubbed the drip from her nose.

'Why didn't you say anything?' She screamed and stomped around the table to stand in front of Olga.

Olga bowed her head and Sarah noticed her hands tremble. 'I…I didn't know how t…to,' she stuttered quietly.

Rebecca stood with her hands on her hips. She threw her head of long hair dramatically back from her face. 'This is her, everyone,' she said and snarled. 'This is actually my birth mother!'

A deep penetrating silence penetrated the room while Sarah heard everyone's sharp intake of breath.

'Good, God,' Mark whispered.

Margaret was the first to react. She got up from her chair and walked around to the back of Olga's chair. She placed both her hands on Olga's shoulders and said, 'Rebecca, why don't you take a deep breath and I'll get you a nice cup of tea.'

Rebecca leaned towards Olga and waved the letter dangerously close to her nose. 'I don't want any tea,' she yelled. 'I've been waiting for this contact from the adoption register since mam died and it's just arrived in this afternoon's post.'

Olga lifted her head and looked at Rebecca. 'I got mine in the post this morning, too. I simply couldn't believe it,' she said.

'So, why didn't you get in touch?' Rebecca raged. 'Why just come here as though nothing was wrong!'

Sarah saw Olga's face soften and her eyes mist with tears. 'I rang your number but got an answer machine and didn't know how or what to say. And I thought if you were at work then I would try again later this evening,' she said. 'And I came here because I wanted to see you.'

Sarah watched Margaret squeeze Olga's shoulders in support.

Rebecca took a deep breath as if she were going to erupt again but then suddenly seemed to lose all her strength and slumped down deflated onto a chair. Her face twisted in confusion, and she stared at Olga. 'Why didn't you want me?' she whimpered. 'Why did you give me away?'

Shrugging Margaret's hands away, Olga stood up. Beads of sweat stood on her forehead and her cheeks were bright red. 'I couldn't. He wouldn't let me,' she shouted and then glared at Ayesha sitting at the other end or the table.

'You kids! You think you've got the monopoly on having to do something against your will. Well, let me tell you, you haven't!' She shrieked. 'I...I wanted to keep my baby, but my father wouldn't let me. I'd disgraced the family and I was shut away for months in a London nursing home. All alone, sixteen years old, and pregnant!'

Grabbing her coat, she stormed towards the door and hurried from the room.

Rebecca got up but Margaret squeezed her arm and pushed her back into the chair. 'Not now, take some time out. I'll go after her,' she said calmly heading to the door. 'Ayesha, use your key, honey, I'll see you later.'

Mark made his way around to Rebecca and put his arms around her. She threw herself into his chest and sobbed. 'Oh, Mark,' she cried. 'All these weeks I've been trying to trace her, and she'd been here in this room all the time and I didn't know.'

'I know,' he soothed clumsily. 'There, there. It'll be alright.'

Jason stood up draping his satchel across his chest. 'Jeez, and I thought I had problems,' he said then waved to Ayesha. He wished everyone a Merry Christmas and quietly left the room.

Ayesha draped her sari over her shoulder and thanked Sarah for the extra vouchers then slipped silently out behind Jason.

Rebecca found a tissue in her bag and blew her nose while Mark let go of her.

'Look, go home, Rebecca,' he said. 'Have a large glass of wine and a soak in the bath. Give yourself time to get used to the idea before you do anything else.'

Rebecca nodded and apologised to Sarah for the upset.

Sarah smiled. 'It's nothing,' she said sympathetically. 'I can't begin to imagine what you are going through.'

Collecting her paperwork, she heard Mark offering to drive Rebecca home who gratefully accepted. They both collected their vouchers and wishing Sarah a Happy Christmas left her alone in the room.

Sarah started to clear away all the samples into a rubbish bag and thought how strange life was. She shook her head in disbelief. To think mother and estranged daughter had been sitting in the same room and didn't know anything about each other. But there again, she supposed, in a small northern town it wasn't unexpected.

She hurried down to her car hoping there was no one associated to her family lurking around in the shadows then tutted at herself.

***

Once Sarah reached home, she instantly felt relaxed and smiled looking around at the neutral décor she'd chosen. The walls were painted in a vanilla cream colour and matching silk drapes highlighted the large window and view of the river. She relaxed back into the soft leather settee, kicked her shoes off onto the oak wood floor and poured herself a well-earned glass of Chablis.

Her mobile rang and broke the silence. She smiled with recognition at the name of her friend in London.

'Hey, Katie,' she answered. 'How's it going?'

'Well, I'm fine, Sarah, but I had my bag snatched on the tube last week, which was horrible, so I'm stuck without my address book to send cards out this year,' she said.

Sarah sympathised with her and said, 'Would you like me
to drop you an email with everyone's addresses on it?'

She heard Katie sigh with relief. 'Oh, that would be
lovely, thanks. Have you heard from anyone lately?'

'No, not really,' Sarah said. 'I've been too busy, have you
seen anybody?'

'Well, I was out with some friends last week and you'll
never guess who we saw?' Katie didn't wait for an answer
but continued, 'Your ex, Paul,' she said. 'Apparently, the
Italian model kicked him out two months ago and he's been
back in London ever since.'

Sarah's mouth dried. Her heart began to race, and she
hunched her shoulders. 'Oh, really? Look, I'm sorry, Katie,
but I'll have to go there's someone at the door,' she lied and
clicked her mobile shut.

Her hands trembled while she placed the mobile gently
onto the glass coffee table and cried out in the silent room.
How could she have been so stupid? And why did she think
she'd ever be able to trust him again?

Tears pricked her eyes and she gulped at the wine. Light-
headed feelings of relief washed over her as she realised
what a lucky escape she'd just had. She had been so
dangerously close to being taken in by his charm and good
looks, yet again.

She hadn't answered his last email because she'd only
decided yesterday that she would refuse his offer to get
back together and give him another chance. Sniffing the
tears away she dried her eyes and congratulated herself for
making the right decision based upon her feelings alone.

She had weighed up the pros and cons of living in London
opposed to North Shields, and surprisingly had decided that
she did feel happier and more content in her hometown. Her
memories of London life were of happy times but when her
life had fallen apart, she'd wanted nothing more than to be

at home. She had also known that it would be a huge wrench to move away from her family and Christine again. But the major factor in her decision had been that she knew now, beyond all doubt, that she wanted a family of her own.

Getting up from the settee she walked to the desk in the corner of the room and booted-up her laptop. Reading his last email again and how he promised never to tell another lie, she snorted. He was nothing more than a compulsive liar. Tapping the reply key, she wondered exactly how to write what she felt about him but decided not to waste her energy.

Later that night she chatted to Christine. 'And so, I typed your two choice words on the email in bold capitals then sent it,' she said and giggled.

Christine hooted with laughter. 'Well done, you,' she said., 'I've been praying you would make the right decision on your own, and you did.'

Sarah told Christine all about the last taste panel and Rebecca's shocking revelation that Olga was her birth mother and how kind Mark had been to her.

Christine asked, 'And did Mark speak to you?

She sighed. 'Oh, just in general chit-chat, really. He looked so unhappy, which of course is partly my fault. I should have listened to your wise words and not told him anything about Paul.'

'Not necessarily, I think you did what you felt was right and it speaks volumes for your feelings towards him that you couldn't tell lies and continue as normal,' Christine said. 'But I do think you should go around to his shop and talk to him.'

Sarah said, 'Oh, yeah, and what excuse do I use to see him?'

Christine laughed. 'He's crazy about you, there's no excuse needed. Go buy him a Christmas present and just turn up unexpected!'

Chapter Eighteen – Friday 21ˢᵗ December

Olga lay in bed the following morning snuggled under the duvet dreading the start of a new day. She couldn't quite remember how she'd got home last night from the supermarket building. It was as if she had been drunk, and her memory was hazy with effects of the alcohol.

She did, however, remember Margaret helping her inside the house and pouring them both a large measure of brandy. Margaret had gently helped her off with her coat like a child and wrapped a throw around her shoulders.

'I'm not cold,' she'd said. 'I just can't stop shivering and my teeth from chattering which happened years ago when I'd had an anaesthetic.'

'You're in shock, it'll soon settle,' Margaret had said then urged her to sip the brandy. Margaret had stayed with her until she'd drunk another measure of brandy and had pulled herself together.

Rolling onto her side now and staring at the pink rose buds on the wallpaper, she remembered the horrible scene in the taste panel room when Rebecca had screamed and shouted at her.

She still couldn't believe it was her. Her daughter, Rebecca, her little baby girl. She began to sob. She let all the emotions pour out of her that she'd kept in control for years. She slowly repeated the words, her daughter, rolling them around on her tongue to see how they sounded spoken aloud.

They were words that she'd whispered to herself under the bed covers during the first few nights after her birth. She remembered the smell of her baby for the few fleeting minutes she had been allowed to hold her. The ache of love she'd felt tugging in the pit of her stomach and how she had tenderly kissed her mass of curly brown hair. But that was when she'd started to howl like a trapped animal and the nuns had whipped her baby away.

Sighing heavily, she got up and padded downstairs into the kitchen to make breakfast. She thought of Rebecca and how extraordinarily proud she was of her daughter. She was a beautiful, professional woman, obviously of high intellect and had done, what her mother would have called, very well for herself.

Sipping her tea, she remembered the way Rebecca had snarled the words, and this is my birth mother. Olga knew Rebecca must hate her and who could blame her, she reasoned, considering the way she'd found out.

However, she had been equally stunned yesterday when she had opened the letter and saw her name with the local address and realised who she was. Knowing now, in hindsight, she should never have gone to the taste panel, but she'd just felt so desperate to see Rebecca. She had wanted to stare at her. Drink her in and examine every detail so she could imagine each year of Rebecca's life that she had missed.

The telephone rang and she answered in her usual manner, 'Olga Treadcott, speaking.'

'Olga, it's me,' Rebecca said. 'I'm terribly sorry about my outburst yesterday. Could I come and talk to you this morning?'

Olga gasped. She wasn't sure if she could cope with any more upset, but Rebecca did sound more in control. She sighed. 'Well, I'm just sort of getting over yesterday, really,' she said. 'And I'm not too sure if I can manage anymore.'

Rebecca said. 'Oh please, Olga. It'll be okay, I've calmed down now, and I just want to talk things through in a more reasonable manner.'

Olga watched Rebecca pull up in her sports car and opened the door welcoming her through into the lounge then excused herself to make coffee. When she re-entered the room Rebecca had sat in Philip's chair opposite to her fireside chair. She could feel her daughter's eyes boring into her back while she placed the tray onto the coffee table.

Rebecca shook her head at the offer of sugar and Olga handed her the coffee which she sipped slowly.

She stared back at her daughter looking for any resemblance to herself but could see none. 'I am sorry about yesterday and you were right I shouldn't have gone to the taste panel as if nothing was wrong,' she said. 'But I was just as shocked as you were and didn't, well I still don't, know how to manage this situation.'

Rebecca continued to stare without speaking so Olga nervously pushed on. 'When I got the letter requesting contact it was a bolt from the blue, to say the least. And I knew there were two options to think about before I made the decision,' she said licking her dry lips. 'I could have chosen option one and declined the contact then continued with my life as normal. Nobody, other than my parents, knew that the dalliance I had with your father, Frank when I was sixteen had produced a child. It was truly scandalous in those days. '

Rebecca sat forward and spoke softly, 'I know after yesterday's behaviour this may be hard for you to believe but I am so grateful that you chose this option. Since I found the adoption papers I have been demented not knowing where I came from and whether I am glad or sad with the outcome this is so much better than not knowing.'

'I suppose it would be,' Olga said nodding. 'I also knew if I chose the second option to contact you, it may turn my entire world upside down. But I never dreamt for one moment that you would be living in the area and in my innocence, or ignorance, I thought I'd be able to write to you first then decide whether to meet or not. And, I say that because of my cowardice and not because I haven't thought about you.'

'So, you have thought about me, then?' Rebecca asked.

Olga looked at her daughter slumped in the chair. She felt tears prick at her eyes and swallowed a huge lump in her throat. 'Oh, Rebecca, of course, I have. I've wondered all my life what you looked like and how your life had turned out. I've prayed every time I set foot into church that you'd been placed with a good family. And I can tell by the way you've talked about your mam in the hospice that she was a good woman. To which I can only thank God.'

Taking a tissue from her sleeve Olga dabbed the wetness from her eyes before continuing. 'Sorry, I don't mean to stare but I'm trying to see if you have any of my family looks but you don't. You are quite simply the double of Frank,' she said.

Rebecca smiled. 'Well, I've counselled myself to listen to your explanations before bombarding you with questions, but I can't keep silent any longer. Please tell me about him and how it all happened?'

Olga relayed the whole story while Rebecca sat looking calm and in control of herself, but Olga could tell she was hanging upon her every word. She made more coffee and insisted upon knowing all about Rebecca's childhood. Her education, her job, her ex-husband and lately her mams illness.

Olga told her all about her late husband, Philip and how she would be spending Christmas Day with Reg at the golf club. She said, 'I know he'd be delighted to have you join us, well, if it's not too early?'

Rebecca smiled. 'I'll think about that,' she said. 'It would be nice to feel I belong somewhere in all of this.'

Chapter Nineteen – Saturday 22nd December

Downloading photographs onto his computer Mark gazed out of the studio window at the Christmas shoppers hurrying up and down the high street. Christmas lights hung across the street, and he could hear the hushed tones of The Salvation Army band playing carols. Sarah's pretty face came into his mind, and he sighed remembering how lovely their kisses had been.

Her lips had been so soft and yielding but at the same time he'd known there was an underlying passion hidden beneath them. He remembered how excited and turned-on he had felt on their first date being lose to such a special woman. And she was special, he thought. She was clever, kind, and had a great sense of humour which surprisingly matched his own, which was a rarity. But now he had lost her.

He was missing her already and knowing he wouldn't see her again this Thursday filled him with abject misery. She would be planning her trip down to London to see Paul for Christmas, he thought. He sincerely hoped she had proof that Paul had changed before she went hurtling back to him. Because even though he hated losing her, it would be awful to see her badly hurt again.

Ellen popped her head around the door. 'Hey, how's the download coming along?'

'Okay, nearly done,' he said. 'Have you got the framed pictures ready for collection this afternoon?'

She perched on a stool next to him. 'Of course, I have,' she said. 'What's up Pop's? You look really fed up?'

He tried to smile but she probed him with her intense stare. He relented and told her all about Sarah and what had happened.

'So, is she going back to him, then?'

He shrugged his shoulders. 'I don't know. She said that she had some serious thinking to do.'

'What!' Ellen cried. 'So, you don't know if she's going to London for certain?'

'Well, she's bound to. She told me how young, good-looking, and gorgeous Paul is,' he said and looked down at himself. 'There's no comparison, is there?'

Ellen gave him a lop-sided grin and gently rubbed his arm. 'You don't know that. And if she thought you were such an old dork, she wouldn't have gone out with you in the first place, now, would she?'

The shop door opened, and they both looked up to see Rebecca standing at the counter.

Mark went to her, and she kissed him briefly on the cheek. 'How are you?' he asked quietly.

'I'm fine,' she said smiling at him. 'I just wanted to call and thank you for helping me on Thursday night. I was in such a state I couldn't have driven myself home.'

Mark ushered her towards the stools in the photography area. 'Here, take a seat for a moment,' he said. 'Ellen was just going to make us coffee.'

She sat down and Mark pulled another stool next to her while Ellen disappeared into the back room.

He said, 'It was more than understandable you'd had such a terrible shock. Have you managed to talk to Olga?'

Rebecca nodded. 'Oh, yeah, I called to see her the next morning and we somehow managed to talk it all through. She told me about my father, Frank and how she'd loved him. But at the age of sixteen she was banished away to have me and then forced to marry her husband, Philip. He was from the same upper-class society as her parents and was deemed a good, respectable match for her.'

Mark nodded gravely. 'The class system in this country has a lot to answer for,' he said.

'Too true,' she said. 'I will try and trace Frank but don't hold out much hope. Olga has little to go on, and well, I'm not sure I've the strength for much more.'

'Well, no wonder you haven't. Why not give yourself a break for the time being, you've been through so much lately. Grieve over your mam properly and then try to get to know Olga a little first,' he said then smirked. 'She might not be as bad as you think?'

Rebecca gave him a playful push on the arm. 'She's not actually,' she said. 'When I saw her name on the letter, I couldn't bear to think that out of all the women I knew it had to be her! And, in the panel group every week I thought she was just a down and out snob, but I have seen a different side to her now. Most days, she is crippled with arthritic pain although you never hear her complain and she reckons it's the pain that makes her so crabby.'

Mark raised an eyebrow.' Hmm,' he said. 'That could be it.'

'Well, that's her excuse anyway,' Rebecca said laughing.

Ellen arrived with coffee and handed them both a mug.

Rebecca wrapped her hands around the mug and sipped the hot coffee. 'Oh, that's good,' she said. 'So, how's it going with you and Sarah?'

Ellen perched on the end of the counter swinging her legs. 'It's not,' she said then explained briefly what had happened.

Mark tutted at Ellen. 'Em, did anyone invite you to join in our conversation?'

'No,' Ellen said. 'But you're obviously not going to do anything about the situation.'

Rebecca cried, 'But you must find out if she's going back to him. For all you know she could have turned him down!'

Ellen nodded at Rebecca with a smug look on her face. 'That's exactly what I told him.'

'Hey,' he shouted. 'This isn't fair, I'm being ganged up on here.'

Rebecca said. 'You have to find out, Mark, you owe it to yourself.'

***

Mark stood outside Sarah's house and looked up at the lights blazing in the lounge. Well, at least she's home, he thought, getting out of the car. He had a small carrier bag in his hand with a Christmas present and he nervously bit on his bottom lip. This was probably going to be the biggest humiliation of his life but as Ellen and Rebecca had told him at least he would know for sure. Taking a deep breath, he rang the doorbell.

***

Sarah jumped up from the settee and looked out of the window to see Mark standing on her doorstep. Her heart started to thump while she hurried to the door wishing she wasn't wearing her old tracksuit and had at least a smidgen of make-up on her face, but she hadn't.

'Hiya,' he said when she opened the door.

She grinned at him. 'Hello, come in,' she said. 'What a lovely surprise to see you.'

She wondered if he could see her heart pumping through the fine gym vest, she wore. The sight of his familiar face made her stomach churn with happiness.

'I just wanted to call and say goodbye properly before you left and because of Rebecca's upset on Thursday night I didn't get a chance,' he said and followed her into the lounge.

She sat down and he perched on the opposite end of the leather settee.

'Before I leave?' she asked raising an eyebrow.

He stared at her. 'Yeah, before you go back down to London to Paul?'

She nodded slowly. 'Ah, but I'm not going back to Paul. I made my decision not to give him another chance,' she said. 'You see, I don't love him anymore.'

'You don't?' He cried, 'So, you're not going back to him?'

She smiled. 'That's right. I'm not going anywhere. I 'm staying right here where I belong.'

***

Mark couldn't believe his ears; she'd just said she didn't love the tosspot anymore. Halleluiah, he thought, she wasn't going back to him, and he might, just might be in with another chance.

She looked flushed, warm, and so lovely that he could feel his knees trembling. He tried to act like the grown man he was but couldn't help feeling like a giddy teenager. He grinned then jumped up from the settee, took both her hands in his and pulled her up onto her feet whirling her around in a spin.

'Sarah, that's the best news I've had for days!'

She burst out laughing when he whooped for joy and they both fell back down onto the settee catching their breath.

She said, 'Well, I was going to call tomorrow to see you in the shop and explain my decision. But after I'd upset you that night in the pub, I wasn't sure what reception I'd get?'

He apologised. 'Look, I'm sorry about being pathetic that night I was just so disappointed,' he said knowing this was his chance. If he hung back now, he'd run the risk of losing her again and that he couldn't bear.

He took a deep breath. 'You see, I know we've only had a couple of dates, but I've fallen for you in a big way,' he said.

Unable to resist her any longer he put his hand into the back of her hair and caressed the nape of her neck.

'You have?' She croaked. 'I thought I'd blown it and when I saw you in the panel room and you could hardly bear to look at me, I didn't think you were interested anymore.'

He stopped her words by briefly kissing her lips. 'You could never blow it with me,' he said. 'I couldn't bear to look at you because I wanted to beg you not to go back to him and that wouldn't have been fair.'

***

The touch of his hand made her tingle from her neck down to her legs. She remembered the first time they'd touched and relished in the same glorious feeling. His face filled her with happiness, and she decided how well he suited his name, Mark. It was steady, reliable, and trustworthy. She loved the sound of his voice when he talked, and she knew there and then she wanted nothing more than to be by his side.

'Oh, right,' she muttered snuggling into his broad chest while he wrapped his big arms around her. She could feel his goatee beard tickling her forehead and sighed in contentment. She didn't need trendy London life; all she needed was him. 'It's you I want to be with, Mark,' she said.

He sat up and put both his hands onto her cheeks. They looked deeply into each other's eyes and kissed long and slow. She slid her arms around his neck, and he scooped her up into his arms then carried her through into the bedroom.

If you have enjoyed this story - A review on amazon.co.uk would be greatly appreciated.

You can find more from Susan Willis here:

An award-winning food lover's romance novel, 'NO CHEF, I Won't!   https://amzn.to/3jefd0M

A psychological suspense novel, Dark Room Secrets
https://amzn.to/3q9jl1M
An award-winning novella with Free recipes inside,
Northern Bake Off https://amzn.to/2Ni4xQy

Website www.susanwillis.co.uk
Twitter @SusanWillis69
Facebook m.me/AUTHORSusanWillis
Instagram susansuspenseauthor
pinterest.co.uk/williseliz7/